Praise for
ALL THE NAMES
THEY USED FOR GOD

"Gripping . . . The nine stories in Anjali Sachdeva's debut collection *All the Names They Used for God* aren't your typical narratives. Each one provides a haiku-esque glimpse into the infinite mind of an individual while revealing how the seeming trivialities of life can reverberate with meaning. Throughout, characters grapple with predetermination as they experience the brutal clash between expectation and reality. . . . Sachdeva mixes the mesmerizing with the petrifyingly dangerous, and the sweet spot nestled at this intersection encapsulates the world in which her characters function. . . . Sachdeva's stories . . . tackle the reader with their totality. Her literary world is magnetic. The author has created perfect, complete microuniverses that lure the reader in to the dark depths of literature like siren song. And yet *All the Names They Used for God* shines in a way that leads characters and readers alike back out of the caves and frozen waters and into the warm, mysterious light."

—*Los Angeles Review of Books*

"Terrific . . . Ms. Sachdeva's book, a debut, is notable for its exuberant variety. . . . There's an element of whimsy to this assortment. . . . The range of her gifts is best seen in the title story, about two young women who are forced to become child brides to Islamists but gradually turn the tables on their captors through the practice of mind control. . . . The story's delicate sadness mingles beautifully with the boldness of its conception."

—*The Wall Street Journal*

"Strange and captivating . . . It's a bizarre kind of normalcy. You can imagine living in this world. And that's what makes this short story work and others like it in Anjali Sachdeva's new book, *All the Names They Used for God.*"

—AUDIE CORNISH, NPR, on the story "Manus"

"Anjali Sachdeva's captivating debut collection, *All the Names They Used for God,* is a gloriously mystifying thrill. These nine unconventional stories resist ready classification or summarization. Most of them seem to float in time, untethered by commercial or cultural touchstones, making them feel eternal, events that could have taken place 150 years ago or yesterday or could happen next year. . . . Sachdeva's creativity is apparently so unbounded that her writing can and does go anywhere. . . . The title story is perhaps the most shatteringly powerful."

—*AM New York*

"Another new and equally impressive voice this season is Anjali Sachdeva, whose debut story collection *All the*

Names They Used for God sprawls all over the usual territories of the genre, from the heartbreaking contemporary urgency of girls kidnapped by Boko Haram (the title story and in many ways the most wrenching piece in the collection) to the comparative rarity of historical science fiction. . . . Sachdeva's stories almost seem to revel in their diversity; the book has surprises on virtually every page and touches on a host of philosophical and technological questions that feature both in the treatises Milton read (and wrote) and today's headlines. Science fiction has always been at its strongest when working exactly this kind of combination, and Sachdeva's first attempts at it are remarkable."

—*The Christian Science Monitor*

"While the nine short stories in Anjali Sachdeva's debut collection don't necessarily belong to the horror genre, there's a merciless quality to them that will haunt readers long after the last page has turned. Spanning realism, science fiction, and everything in between, Sachdeva creates unique, convincing, and often gut-wrenching worlds in each of her pieces. Her richly-crafted characters—from two Boko Haram kidnapping victims forging new lives to humans faced with alien overlords who demand they replace their hands with metal prosthesis—will keep readers on their toes and the edge of their seats."

—*Harper's Bazaar*

"Are you ever-so-slightly bitter that you, an adult, are supposed to have outgrown fairy tales by now? Don't worry—thanks to Sachdeva's debut short story collection, you can have fairy tales for grown-ups. The stories in *All the Names They Used for God* are myths told in spare, but effective, sentences. Even if they're set in the modern day, each imagines a world in which the possibility for magic isn't entirely ruled out."

—*Refinery29*

"So rich they read like dreams . . . the nine stories in Sachdeva's otherworldly debut center upon the unforgiving forces that determine the shape of our lives, as glorious as they are brutal. . . . The stories that follow span time, space, and logic: Nigeria and New Hampshire, the past and the future, realism and science fiction. And yet, for all its scope, it is a strikingly unified collection, with each story reading like a poem, or a fable, staring into the unknowable. . . . They are enormous stories, not in length but in ambition, each an entirely new, unsparing world. Beautiful, draining—and entirely unforgettable."

—*Kirkus Reviews* (starred review)

"A wide-ranging collection of stories that are a blend of fact and fiction, seamlessly integrating magical realism and the firmly earthbound . . . Sachdeva's spare, unsentimental writing is never more artfully deployed than in the title story, an emotionally scorching tale of two African women's kidnap and escape from a Boko Haram–type army. . . . Sachdeva's eclectic stories span time and geography, packing a wallop even greater due to their diversity. It's a strong collection from start to finish, with not a weak story in the bunch."

—*BookPage*

"In addition to their incisive characterization and fluid prose, the stories are united by a bold thematic exploration of the unknown."

—*Tin House*

"Perfect short story collections are not unlike perfect albums. Just as Fleetwood Mac's *Rumours* or Bob Dylan's *Blood on the Tracks,* varied in style though their tracks may be, cohere to express a certain sentiment (if not a narrative), so too do the stories in the perfect collection buttress each other so that the whole is more than the sum. And, as rare as a perfect album may be, perhaps the perfect short story collection is even rarer. . . . Yet every so often, a single-author short story collection is published that's the equivalent of *Kind of Blue* or *Graceland,* a narrative tone poem where the assembled stories in their diversity and difference serve to tell an overreaching story in that mysterious and subtle way that only a perfect assemblage can. Such is the case with Anjali

Sachdeva's brilliant debut collection, *All the Names They Used for God*. Sachdeva's stories break down barriers between genres, from magical realism, to American gothic, to science fiction. . . . Sachdeva is the sort of fabulist who rejects the simplicities of allegory; her characters have a bit of the mythic about them but are never simply symbols. . . . That sense of significance through mystery makes the stories feels intoxicated with faith, but a very idiosyncratic, cracked kind of faith. . . . Some writers have their little corner of the world; Sachdeva has the entire world."

—*The Rumpus*

"Striking . . . The nine stories range from more or less realistic to ambiguously dreamlike, from visionary historical fiction to outright fantasy. Each story introduces a unique new world through which Ms. Sachdeva guides readers with a sure hand and imagination burning bright. . . . Whether it is realistic or speculative, Anjali Sachdeva's work is like the best science fiction or fantasy, forcing readers to consider the world anew, even as it entertains deliciously."

—*Pittsburgh Post-Gazette*

"Anjali Sachdeva's nine-story collection, *All the Names They Used for God,* is filled with surreal stories grounded in reality. A comparison is *Black Mirror,* the TV sci-fi anthology

show that explores the dangers of technology when it's deeply integrated into our lives. Similar to the show, Sa deva is fascinated with exploring how large-scale mo ments like technology and religion impact our human She sets her stories all over countries and eras, from a p neer prairie farm to modern day Africa, and occasiona casts her reader into the future. The stories usually beg under the premise of normalcy, but slowly and deft Sachdeva weaves in something other."

—*Electric Literatu*

"[A] striking debut short story collection . . . enchanting ar mesmerizing . . . Sachdeva's writing is carefully texture and nuanced. Each key scene . . . is also unfolded at ju the right pace. . . . Reminiscent of Aimee Bender's an Kelly Link's excellent speculative works."

—*PopMatter*

"This phenomenal debut short story collection is filled witl stories that bring the other-worldly to life and examine th strangeness of humanity."

—*Bustle*

"This ambitious debut short-story collection spans centuries and continents in its panorama of characters in pursuit of the sublime."

—*Entertainment Weekly*

touch such red-hot stories on the other side of the globe. I admire Sachdeva's verve, and I can't wait to see what's next."

—*The Christian Century*

"The nine stories in Sachdeva's intriguing debut collection raise challenging questions about human responses to short-circuited desires. Equally at home in realistic and speculative plots, Sachdeva crafts precise character studies with minimal flourishes. . . . Some stories are creative riffs on historic events, including the title story, in which two kidnapping victims of Boko Haram discover a quasimagical form of hypnosis that can control men. Others, such as 'Manus,' point to alarming futures, in which aliens have conquered earth without upsetting life too much—other than requiring all humans replace their hands with metal prosthetics. The most affecting story, 'Pleiades,' updates the hubris of Greek tragedy: the inexplicable illnesses of genetically modified septuplets undercut their parents' faith in science. Throughout, characters face a perpetual constraint against full expression of their emotions. These inventive stories will challenge readers to rethink how people cope with thwarted hopes."

—*Publishers Weekly*

"What an outstanding short story collection. I knew nothing about this book going in and was thrilled by each story.

There is so much range here, and there is a nice fabulist edge to nearly all the stories. The writer wields so much confidence and control in her prose, and my goodness, what imagination, what passion there is in this work. From one story to the next I felt like the writer knows everything about everything. One of the best collections I've ever read. Every single story is a standout."

—ROXANE GAY

"*All the Names They Used for God* fuses science, myth, and imagination into a dark and gorgeous series of questions about our current predicaments. Sachdeva is a fascinating storyteller, willing to push her inventiveness as far as it will go, and I cannot wait to see what she writes next."

—ANTHONY DOERR, Pulitzer Prize–winning author of *All the Light We Cannot See*

"Every once in a while you read a book with such power, craft, and originality, you know instantly that a new and important voice has arrived on the scene. This is that book."

—KAREN JOY FOWLER, *New York Times* bestselling author of *We Are All Completely Beside Ourselves* and *The Jane Austen Book Club*

"With this book Anjali Sachdeva moves literature forward a notch and moves the short story form a full revolution.

Yes, it's that good—fresh, original, and moving. The prose is gorgeous and the characters still linger with me. I love this book."

—CHRIS OFFUTT, author of
My Father, the Pornographer and
Kentucky Straight: Stories

"Anjali Sachdeva is a sorcerer, and these stories are magic. They are so skillfully told, and so absorbing, that they pass as swiftly as a song, yet they linger in the memory like a novel. I read them with total immersion and delight, and not a little envy."

—KEVIN BROCKMEIER, author of
The Illumination

**Praise for "Pleiades," anthologized in
The Best American Nonrequired Reading, 2011**

"Sometimes we read things that are okay. Sometimes we read things that we find important in some way—that we learn from, but that don't particularly get us all riled up. And sometimes we read something that just astounds and grabs and makes its way into the bones of everyone in the class. . . . The story seemed to me some kind of small masterpiece. . . . I went home feeling electric about the possibility of the written word."

—DAVE EGGERS, *The Washington Post*

ALL THE NAMES
THEY USED FOR GOD

SPIEGEL & GRAU

NEW YORK

ALL THE NAMES
THEY USED FOR GOD

STORIES

Anjali Sachdeva

2019 Spiegel & Grau Trade Paperback Edition

Published in the United States by Spiegel & Grau, an imprint of Random House, a division of Penguin Random House LLC, New York.

SPIEGEL & GRAU and colophon is a registered trademark of Penguin Random House LLC.

Originally published in hardcover and in slightly different form in the United States by Spiegel & Grau, an imprint of Random House, a division of Penguin Random House LLC, in 2018.

The following stories have been previously published: "The World by Night" in *The Iowa Review,* "Glass-lung" in *The Yale Review,* "Robert Greenman and the Mermaid" in *Alaska Quarterly Review,* "Manus" in *The Literary Review,* and "Pleiades" in *Gulf Coast.*

LIBRARY OF CONGRESS CATALOGUING-IN-PUBLICATION DATA
Names: Sachdeva, Anjali, author.
Title: All the names they used for God: stories / Anjali Sachdeva
Description: New York: Spiegel & Grau, 2018.
Identifiers: LCCN 2017027249 | ISBN 9780525508687 (trade paperback) | ISBN 9780525508670 (ebook)
Subjects: | BISAC: FICTION / Short Stories (single author). | FICTION / Literary.
Classification: LCC PS3619.A275 A6 2018 | DDC 813/.6—dc23
LC record available at lccn.loc.gov/201702727249

Printed in the United States of America on acid-free paper

spiegelandgrau.com
randomhousebooks.com

2 4 6 8 9 7 5 3 1

Illustrations on pages 106, 166, and 232: © iStockphoto.com

Book design by Dana Leigh Blanchette

FOR MY DAUGHTERS,

NAMED FOR MYSTERY AND WISDOM;
MAY LIFE OFFER YOU
SOME OF BOTH.

Crossing a bare common, in snow puddles, at twilight, under a clouded sky, without having in my thoughts any occurrence of special good fortune, I have enjoyed a perfect exhilaration. I am glad to the brink of fear.

—RALPH WALDO EMERSON,
"NATURE"

Contents

Introduction

In the old times, people knew better than to trust the gods. Deities were tempestuous, even capricious. They could bring harvest or drought, make your mouth drip with jewels or snakes, and their reasons were often mysterious. People lived accordingly; they expected a measure of bitterness with anything sweet.

But who can be bothered, these days, with the kinds of gods who would sucker punch you when you weren't looking, or stumble in drunk halfway through Thanksgiving dinner and demand sacrifices? We want dependable deities, a God whose love you can sing pop songs about. We want benevolence, mercy, white light, guaranteed two-day shipping. And if the gods can't offer it, we can look elsewhere:

to science, nature, psychology, industry—massive forces defined by clear rules and logic.

Or so we convince ourselves, right up until our new gods start to misbehave. Powers that far outstrip our understanding can wound us with the slightest touch, and they'd be pale gods if they couldn't. If we're honest with ourselves, that risk is what draws us to them—to witness the glory of wild nature, the unfettered power of chemistry or biology, the brush with the sublime that can uplift or wither us with equal ease. Wonder and terror meet at the horizon, and we walk the knife-edge between them.

ALL THE NAMES
THEY USED FOR GOD

THE WORLD BY NIGHT

Sadie was sixteen when her parents died, and the grave-digger told her he would charge her less if she'd help him. Typhoid had killed so many people in town that he was tired of digging.

"Can we do it at night?" she asked. Her skin could not weather the long hours in the sun, and in the glare of day she would be nearly blind.

He agreed, and so there they were, twilight 'til dawn, shaving slivers of hard-packed earth from the walls of the graves. They had the coffins lowered by morning and the gravedigger looked at Sadie's flushed face and said, "Go on and get inside now. I'll finish this. I'll do it proper. You can have your own service tonight."

"Aren't you afraid of me?" she asked. She'd been wanting to ask all night. When she was tired or nervous her irises often jumped back and forth uncontrollably, as though she were being shaken, and she knew they were doing so now. It unsettled people, and more than one preacher had tried to cast spirits out of her, to no effect.

The gravedigger looked at the earth for a long time, the pits with the bodies resting at the bottoms. "I saw another girl like you once, at a freak show in Abilene," he said. "White skin and hair like yours, eyes like I never saw, almost violet. They called her the Devil's Bride, but I think she would've liked to've been married to a good man, tending chickens and baking biscuits just like anyone else. Anyhow, you're a fine digger."

Now Sadie is twenty and it is June and her husband Zachary has been gone for two months, moving southeast across the Ozarks and maybe farther, to look for work. She is not afraid of being alone. She was alone for two years before she met Zachary and she had thought she would spend the rest of her life that way. Just knowing he will come back sooner or later is enough.

She sleeps in the sod house through the bright hours of the day when most women do their chores, saves her work for early morning and dusk. When the dark has settled she walks across the prairie, making her way by scent and feel. She finds some clumps of grass that smell like onion, others like sweet basil, others still covered in silvery down that tickles her fingertips.

As the days pass, she saves up things to tell Zachary about when he comes home: A patch of sweet blackberries by the side of the pond where she draws the wash water. A hollow where a covey of grouse nest. Most important and mysterious of all, a hole in the ground with nothing but darkness inside, about the size of a barrel top. The grasses there move even when there is no breeze, and the hole breathes cool air. Once, she lowered a lantern into it at the end of her clothesline and saw a slope of jagged stone leading down. She stuck her head into the opening and breathed, and the air smelled just like the walls of her parents' graves.

When Sadie first met Zachary it was dusk and he was drunk. She was sweeping the front steps of the house she had lived in with her parents, and had a pot of elderberry jam boiling on the stove inside. A man stopped at the gate and said, "Appaloosa." Sadie kept sweeping, but the word brought to mind the horses, stark white with a dappling of dark spots, that the Indians rode across the plains. "Appaloosa," the man said again. "Appaloosa, I'm talking to you." He sauntered up to her and took her face in his hand, fumes of whiskey and turpentine exuding from his clothes. He had straight black hair to his shoulders and fingers that were strong and calloused. Sadie stood very still as he rubbed her chin with his thumb, then showed her the dark purple smear of elderberry juice that stained it.

"Not real spots at all," he said. "You're in disguise. You must be one of those Arab horses like the kings and queens ride, white from head to shoes." He licked his thumb clean. Sadie didn't say anything, just tightened her grip on the broom handle, but he dropped his hand and stepped back and bowed to her lightly. "I'll see you tomorrow," he said, and just as quickly as he'd appeared, he was gone.

She finished sweeping the steps and went inside. Looking in the glass, she could see that her whole pale face was spotted with the dark juice, her hands, too. She wiped herself clean with a damp cloth and went back to the canning, not thinking she'd ever see the man again. But he did come back the next day, and knocked on the door like any gentleman. The sound startled Sadie awake in her parents' old feather bed, and she crept into the living room in her nightgown. Through the curtains she could just make out the shape of a man walking away down the front path. When she cracked the door open, there was a handful of dusty flowers on the stairs and a note. The grocer read it for her later: "My name is Zachary Pollard and I live at the boardinghouse by the bank and this is a gift for you."

He came every day after that, too, though once he learned better, he came in the evening, and they sat on the porch steps with a candle between them and talked. Her parents had been dead two years and he was the first person since their death to speak to her about anything more important than the weather or the cost of flour. He was, he liked to say, mostly orphan himself. His mother was a Chinook Indian, but she had died when he was a boy and now he had nothing left of her but her songs and her language and a fine beaded bangle that he kept wrapped in a handkerchief at the bottom of his trunk. His father was a Scotch-Irish peddler whom he had not seen in a dozen years. None of this seemed to sadden him. Though he was only twenty, he had a hundred thrilling stories to tell, had traveled much of the country and met all manner of people. "But none like you, Appaloosa," he would say. Sadie had often wished she looked like everyone else, but after she met Zachary she stopped wishing it. He drank her in with his eyes as though the very sight of her were delightful.

She worried it would not last. During the months when she and Zachary were courting, she was convinced every day that he would change his mind and leave her. The day they were married she held his arm so tight she left crimps in the fabric of his shirt, and to put the ring on her finger he had to pry her loose.

By the time the last hot days of summer come, she is restless. Even the weather seems impatient. Great masses of blue-black cloud gather above the prairie, and lightning cracks sideways at the horizon while the wind sets her hair whipping about her face. Times like these the world feels more alive than any other, like she is only a mosquito resting on the hide of some great beast.

But when the storms end, the stillness is intolerable. She opens Zachary's trunk and riffles the pages of his few small books between her fingers, wishing for the thousandth time that she could read them. She left school at eight when the

schoolmistress complained that she was too much of a distraction to the other children, and that she still had not
managed to learn her letters. When Sadie failed to learn
them even from her mother, her parents took her to a doctor, who said her eyes were weak in a way he could not fix,
that she was oversensitive to light, and farsighted; she would
not learn to read and probably would not be much of a
seamstress. He gave her a pair of dark glasses and sent her
home. Standing on her front porch, Sadie hooked the
glasses over her ears and looked at the people and horses
moving through the artificial dusk the glass created. Brilliant bits of light still stabbed in from the sides of the lenses,
and, though she could see better, people stared at her even
more than they had before.

She sets the books aside and carefully unpacks the rest of
the trunk. Here is the shirt Zachary was married in, a spare
horse blanket, a bundle of coins, a wrinkled handkerchief
folded in neat quarters, and a long coil of rope. Sadie un-
winds it and feels the whole length to satisfy herself that it
is sound, and, finding it so, she coils it again. From beside
the stove she takes the stout iron bar she uses to stir the fire.
She slips a handful of matches into her dress pocket. With
the iron bar in one hand and the lantern and rope in her
other, she goes outside.

She moves as quickly as she can to the cave entrance and
ties one end of the rope to the iron bar, then hammers the
bar into the earth with a stone until she believes it will hold

her weight. After one last tug on the rope, she steps gingerly into the mouth of the cave and begins the steep descent.

Once she has reached the floor, the opening to the cave blazes above her like a jagged red sun, but around her all is cool and dim. The lantern light does not go far in darkness this profound, but by moving around the perimeter of the space she soon gains its measure.

At one end of the room she finds a tunnel, big enough to scuttle through at a crouch, and decides to see where it leads. As she goes farther, the passage angles steeply downward and grows narrower, until there is barely room for her to crawl and none to turn around. She has a sudden urge to stand up, though she knows she can't. The stone floor cuts against her knees. She has no sense of how far she has come, and for all she knows the tunnel might end in a blank wall, and if it does, she will have to crawl the whole way backward, if she can even do such a thing. The panic makes her muscles twitch; she has to force herself to pause and breathe deeply to stay her own frantic motion. She imagines she is at home, in the little corner of the house where they store the potatoes, where the earthen walls squeeze close around her. At last she is calmer and moves forward again, and soon the tunnel widens out into another room. Sadie stands and stretches, claps her hands. To her right the sound echoes back, quick and sharp, but to the left it fades away into nothing. She sings out a line from her favorite hymn, "Glory, glory, praise His name," and the stone walls sing back to her in a weird chorus. Laughing, she sings to the end of the song and holds her breath as the echoes fade. This is her reward for pushing herself forward when she might have turned back. She has never been anywhere so strange and apart from the world. It feels as though this place belongs to her alone, and before she has even begun the crawl back up through the tunnel, she knows she will return.

All through autumn she visits the cave almost every day. Most times she goes only to the room at the bottom of the rope and lies in the cool darkness, breathing in the moist air. She daydreams, thinks sometimes of her parents, but most often tries to trace Zachary's progress in her mind, imagine where he is and what he might be doing.

The day before he left the two of them had gone for a ride in the early evening, the prairie still pale green and tender then, and if she tries she can sometimes summon the feel of his arm around her waist, his chest against her back as he let the horse wander through the tall grasses.

"Will you be all right?" he'd said. "It'll be a long while."

"I can wait."

"Go to the Burkes if you have any trouble."

"I won't. She always looks at me like I'm a bug. I'd rather starve to death."

"Well, I'd rather you didn't. I'm worried about leaving you alone."

"Don't go, then. I'm the one with cause to worry, with you so far away."

He laughed, but it was a sad laugh. "I used to be a wild thing, you know, before I met you. I've drunk toasts in places that would make your stomach turn. I can take care of myself."

"I can take care of you, too," she said.

He sighed and kissed her neck, and turned the horse gently back to home.

Some days she ventures through the tunnel, into the larger room, and beyond. She takes with her cloth scraps that she ties as markers so she will not lose her way, and the farther she explores, the more wonders she discovers. In some places streams of icy water cut through the caves, and after spending many long minutes staring into the current she notices the darting movement of small white fish and crayfish throwing back the light of her lantern. In other places she finds chimneys in the rock that seem to drop down forever, and empty riverbeds where the stone feels like melted glass. Pale crickets chirp from hidden niches. Every room holds some new wonder, and the joy of discovery stokes in her a boldness she has never felt in the world above. Her only regret is that Zachary is not with her. She knows he believes he has seen everything the world has to offer, but he has never seen anything like this.

Then, too soon, the first snowfall comes. Sadie presses her nose against the tiny frosted window of the sod house and watches the flakes cover the bleached prairie. Within a day the snow reaches her knees, and soon after it is covered by a crust of ice. The glare of sunlight on the vast expanse of white is blinding at any hour of the day, and Sadie can't find the entrance to the cave anymore now that the snow has erased all the features of the land. Bound indoors, she cleans, or cooks, or sings to herself. Despite what the doctor told her parents, she has learned to sew well enough, feeling the stitches and the way the fabric comes together with the tips of her fingers, so she busies herself patching the holes in her winter coat. Nights are so bitter she can't bear to be outdoors very long, but when the sky is unclouded she wraps herself in her quilt and lies in the snow looking at the riot of stars that fills every inch of the sky, so clear she feels she could prick her face against them if she stood up too quickly.

Still, this is not enough to take up much time, and she begins to think she may go crazy in the little sod house. The winter before, Zachary read to her through the long hours, and sang while she played the guitar, and sometimes held on to her silently in their little bed, so quietly that she thought he was asleep until some slight movement made him hold her more tightly. Without him, the days are too long. She does not care to visit the Burkes, and the next homestead past them is ten miles distant. Soon she begins to sleep for long portions of the day, and the night, too.

At last some travelers come by, a man and a woman and a baby. Sadie sees the shadow of their wagon move past the window, and goes quickly to the door to call to them. They come in stamping the snow from their feet and smiling, but a stricken look passes across their faces when they see her clearly in the firelight.

"Would you like something to eat?" Sadie says quickly. There is little enough to spare if her stores are to last until spring, but she is desperate for their company. "Maybe it's been a while since you've had a hot meal."

"We can't stop long," says the man.

"Just a cup of tea and some bread, then?"

The couple huddles together at the table as Sadie adds wood to the stove, sets the bread to warm, and boils water for the tea. There is one jar of blackberry preserves left and she puts that on the table as well. She slips her glasses on. They are more of a hindrance than a help inside the house, but she can hear the travelers' fear in their voices, and knows the smoked glass will hide the way her eyes shake.

"I can hold the baby while you eat," she says.

"Oh, no," says the woman. "She doesn't take well to other people." She leans the baby against her shoulder and eats hastily with one hand.

When the food is gone, Sadie sees that they mean to go immediately, and it fills her with a sense of dread so keen she nearly grabs the woman's hand where it rests on the table. Instead she says, "I wonder if you would write something for me?"

The woman nods and hands the baby to her husband.

Sadie takes a pen and ink and paper from Zachary's trunk and sets them on the table. "Only write, 'Dear Zachary, I will be back soon. Love, your Sadie.'"

The woman writes, and when the ink is dry she folds the paper in quarters and hands it to Sadie, keeping her eyes on the tabletop the whole time.

"Thank you."

"No trouble in it," the woman says. "Thank you for the food. We'd best be going."

Sadie watches the wagon disappear against the horizon, though it hurts her eyes to do it. As soon as they are gone, she begins to fill Zachary's old knapsack. She takes the lantern, candles, matches, a shawl, a fat bundle of cloth scraps. She fills the rest of the space with food and a flask of water. Lastly, she slips her coat on and grabs her broom from the fireside and heads out into the prairie, where she stabs at the snow with the broom handle for more than an hour until at last she finds the spot she wants, where the handle plunges deep into the ground. She kicks the snow aside and looks at the iron bar, the icy rope. It is a wild idea, she knows, but she feels wild, trapped in the confines of the house day upon day with no sound except the screaming of the wind.

She reaches the floor of the cave and waits to catch her breath. Already she feels better, more at home. The cave is warmer than the prairie above. Her bag lies at her feet. It holds enough food to last her a week; she can do some real exploring without having to worry about getting back for supper. She lights the lantern and moves carefully to the tunnel that leads to the larger room. Once there, she tries a passage she has not taken before. It proves to be a short tunnel, and after a few minutes of crawling, she is stepping into another vast rock room. The wall to one side is encrusted with a brilliant white froth of minerals that glitters in the light of her lamp. She stands for a long time just looking at the light winking back at her before she brushes the stone with her fingertips, which come away coated in a powdery residue.

Sadie has been exploring for a few hours and has investigated a handful of rooms when she decides to retrace her steps, but finds that she cannot locate her marker. Standing at the entrance to the tunnel she is almost sure she came down, she moves the lantern slowly, patiently, around its dark mouth, but does not see anywhere the strip of bright red flannel that should confirm her way. She takes a deep breath and starts again at the base of the tunnel, feeling the rock with her fingers this time, waiting for the welcome softness of the cloth. Nothing. So she must be mistaken. The room is large and there are a number of tunnels branching from it; she moves to the next one and starts her search again.

Perhaps an hour has passed by the time she has checked all the tunnels she can find, and still there is no marker anywhere. She cannot believe she has forgotten to leave one, but it is just possible, with her excitement and her eagerness to move ahead. Or else she has not found the proper tunnel. Or else the marker was not tied securely, and is lying somewhere on the cave floor. None of which tells her what she should do. She has returned, or thinks she has, to where she started, that first tunnel that she initially felt confident in. She checks its perimeter one last time and then decides she must give this one a try. Soon after she enters it, though, she becomes convinced she has made a mistake. The ceiling is lower than she remembered, the way more twisted. Frustrated, she calls out, and the echo that answers her promises an open space close ahead. As she emerges, impatient, into the next room, her foot plunges into empty air and she falls headlong onto the rock, her lantern rolling ahead of her, the candle quickly extinguished.

Lying with her face to the ground, she feels the floor around her to ensure that it is solid, and pulls her knees to her chest and sobs. There is no way for anyone to find her, unless they were to come across the iron bar and the dangling rope and become curious, but there is little chance of anyone roaming across the land in the winter. Her right knee is scraped raw where she landed on it, as are her hands. She has been foolish, and now she will pay for her foolishness.

Eventually she stops crying. She feels the floor around her until she locates the lantern, gingerly touches the glass panes and finds them unbroken. Her matches are still in her pocket, and she strikes one, relights the candle, and draws a shuddering breath.

She imagines what Zachary would say, and feels ashamed of herself. She has not even looked for a way out. She could cry for days and do nothing more than make herself thirsty. Better to take stock: She has been in the cave for half a day, and has food for a week. So she will have to find another exit. There are small streams running everywhere for water, and she will be sparing with the food until she is sure of her escape route. When she gets home, she will tear up the note she left and Zachary will never even know she was gone.

For a while a sense of certainty buoys her—she finds another passage leading from the room and follows it, confident that she will soon be on the surface. But that tunnel branches into another, and another, and soon she can no longer say which direction she started from.

In the constant darkness, the passage of time becomes impossible to calculate. She knows only that the food in her pack is diminishing, though she allows herself only a bite or two at a time, and stretches the hours between bites as long as she can. How much time has it been? Days, certainly. Weeks, probably, but more than that she can't say. The uneven ground and the danger of falling force her to move slowly, and she eats so little that she grows tired easily. After a while, she begins to crouch by the icy rivers and swipe at the white fish, flipping them from the water to the cave floor, where they thrash until they die and she can rinse them clean and eat them. Their skins are soft and scaleless, their bones fine as grass, but they are small and not much nourishment, and she is plagued by constant, dull hunger.

Sometimes she thinks she hears sounds: snatches of laughter, and a low, hollow whistle like a distant train. There are faces, too, in the dim light of the lamp, looking at her from the corners of the ceilings, and sometimes the sound of something scuttling past behind her, something she is never quick enough to see. She tries to call out, to talk to these fleeting forms, but never receives any answer. More and more often she takes refuge in sleep, the darkness of her closed eyes blending seamlessly with the darkness of her waking hours.

She wakes again and it's indistinguishable from the last hundred times she has woken, except that when she tries to rise the effort feels too great. Her body hurts all the time, and it's hard to remember sometimes what she is looking for. *A door,* she thinks. *I'm looking for the door.* If she stops paying attention for one moment she might find herself plunging into some unnoticed hole in the floor, but attention is hard to come by with the great heavy silence of the cave in her ears and the darkness constantly changing shapes around her. At last, she turns over and pushes herself up on her knees. She crawls through a low slot in the rock wall into a new room and sees something like a snowfall of stars against the far wall, soft blue streaks of light drifting down against the blackness. She laughs and holds out her hand, but realizes the light lies on the other side of a chasm some six feet wide that begins just past her fingertips. She could jump across it, perhaps, but if she misses she is done. So she kneels at the edge, feeling the cool air across her face and watching the drifting pattern of light on black. *It must be nearly Christmas,* she thinks. *Maybe today.* Zachary will be somewhere in a saloon along the road back to her, drinking beer with strangers. Or at a boardinghouse filled with lonely men, all sitting down to roast goose and feeling grateful for a moment of warmth. And maybe not just men. Maybe some pretty young widow is smiling at Zachary, carving a helping of meat onto his plate and setting her hand on his shoulder, leaning too close. Sadie lies on her belly at the edge of the chasm and holds out the lantern to look down. At the bottom there is a distant glow like candlelight. Sadie thinks she can hear voices, and as she listens harder she is sure—a throng of people conversing. Some are laughing, even, and their voices get louder the more she listens. She can almost tell what they are saying, but the walls of the cave distort the sound, keeping it just barely unintelligible. "Hello!" she calls, but they don't answer, don't even pause in their conversation. Maybe they can't hear her. She has noticed that sounds sometimes come from very far away in the cave. Once she thought she heard a lark singing just over her shoulder, but there was nothing around her but blackness.

Sadie calls out to the distant people again, but again there is no response. She lies by the chasm, pulling her fingers through the empty air just past her cheek. Where did all those people come from? What are they doing here? Maybe they live here. Maybe they have never seen the sun in their whole lives and their skin is as white as hers. She imagines a dark room filled with white-skinned men and women, children, babies. White foxes and cats thread between their legs as they stand talking, white birds sing from the crenellations in the walls. There is a long table laid with candles and heaped with food. One of the women is singing, a soft, clear melody that Sadie's mother used to sing to her when she was a child: "And the stars fell through my fingers, Lord." What is it called? She can't remember the name, or the rest of the song. "Zachary," she says, "you are missing the most wonderful party. You are missing so many things. You should be here at home with me."

She wakes hours or minutes later, her cheek resting against the sharp edge of the chasm. A cool updraft still blows past her, but the raining blue light is gone, and the candle she left burning in her lantern has melted away. Where the people were she hears only the muttering of water at the bottom of the crevasse. She feels too tired to move. In her shrunken pack are two candles and a hard lump of brown sugar. *I will stay here until those people come back,* she thinks. *Maybe they're looking for me.* Some part of her knows she is starving, that if she does not find a way out soon she will die here, that she cannot live on icy water and thin-boned fish for much longer. But it is difficult to care.

The darkness feels safe, the hard rock embracing. With the lantern extinguished, her eyes trace luminous patterns against the black, carnivals of moving light more beautiful than anything she can recall from home.

But then she remembers Zachary. He may have been waiting for days, for weeks, whatever time she has been gone. He may have come home as soon as she left, may even now be standing with her letter in his hand and scanning the snow for her long-erased footprints.

She crawls back from the edge of the crevasse and struggles to her feet, reaches into the pack for a candle, but thinks better of it and stands still, listening. *Tell me something,* she says to the cave, and the cave breathes back at her, its million water droplets echoing against its stony heart. She puts the lantern in her pack and begins to move blind, sweeping her toes against the ground, reaching out with her hands to find the walls. There is a smell in the air, barely noticeable, that is different from the rest of the smells. She does not know what it is but she follows it, into tunnels and down slopes and through a crack in the wall so small she has to empty all the air from her lungs to get through. And then she comes around a corner and there is a slash of open space in the rock above her head, and the light burning through it makes her gasp and cover her eyes. When she has recovered from the shock, she can see that the ceiling is only a foot above her. She reaches up through the rent in the stone and feels a frigid wind against her fingertips.

Sadie knows she must pull herself up, but it seems beyond her strength. She sits on the floor and eats her last spoonful of sugar, feels its energy spill into her blood in a way that makes her simultaneously strong and dizzy. At last she puts her pack on the ground, grabs the edges of the opening in the rock, and pulls and kicks toward the light. Soon she is pushing through the snow-crusted skeletons of black-eyed Susans and rolling into the howling flat of the prairie. In the distance she can see the lightning-struck tree that marks the far side of the Burkes' property. She clutches her arms against her chest, turns her back to the wind, and sits a long while with her eyes closed.

When she nears her house, she sees smoke coming from the chimney and bursts through the door. Someone looks up from the bed, startled, and for a moment her heart jumps. But she sees almost instantly that it is not Zachary. This person is fair-haired and slight, wrapped in her wool blanket. He shouts in alarm and drops the piece of wood he was carving.

"Who are you?" she says.

He gapes at her. "I'm sorry. I'm sorry. I'll go."

"Is Zachary here?" she says, but the man just shakes his head.

Sadie is shivering. She looks to the stove, where a pan of coffee steams. Not hers; she ran out before she went into the cave. But if someone sees fit to come into her house and use her things, she will drink his coffee without apology.

She takes her tin cup from the hook and pours what remains into it, blows across the surface and begins to drink. "Who are you?" she says again.

"My name's Jesse Meecham. Are you one of them that lived here?"

"I still do live here. I'd like to know who you think you are, coming into my house." She glances around for her shotgun, spots it in the corner on the other side of the doorway, an easy stride away. She takes another sip of the coffee. The warmth moves through her body. Now that she is back in the house, she is aware of a ravenous hunger she has not felt since her first days underground. She opens the sugar tin and adds a fistful of sugar to the coffee. "You wanted to get out of the snow, I suppose?"

"I was on my way from Springfield, but a storm come up and I lost the track. When I got here there was no one about. I found your note, but after a while when no one come back I figured you was dead."

By his voice he sounds young, maybe only fifteen or sixteen, but the droop of his shoulders gives him a sad and desperate look. He stops talking and reaches out and grabs her arm, holding on firmly but not painfully, watching her face. At last, he lets go and sits back on the bed. He seems less frightened, more watchful. Sadie steps away and takes the gun from the corner.

"You's a real woman, ain't you?" he says. "I thought you was a ghost. What happened to you?"

"Nothing happened. I've been away some time is all."

"Why's your face so pale?"

"Just is."

He stares a moment more, then says, "I've got a bit of salt pork, if you're hungry."

"All right."

The boy gets up from the bed, paws the grounds from the coffee pan, sets it back on the stove and slices the meat into it. Sadie can smell the remnants of the coffee burning seconds before the bacon fat covers them, a smell so warm and vital she feels drunk on it. When the meat is cooked Jesse forks it onto a plate, and Sadie feels every second that passes until it is cool enough to eat, until the warm fat fills her mouth. She empties the plate and says, "My husband won't like you being here. You'll have to leave. I'll point you to the trail."

The boy nods. "S'pose I could wait until morning? The day's mostly gone."

Sadie points with the gun. "You can take that blanket and stretch out by the fire for tonight."

Jesse moves to the fireside and sits huddled in the blanket while she sinks down on the bed. Whatever power got her back across the prairie to home is quickly draining away; she feels as though she could sleep for days. She turns to pull a quilt from the shelf and catches a glimpse of herself in the square of looking glass on the wall. Even she can see that her face is skeletal and dirty; she looks like the starved deer that sometimes wander by in the winter, all ribs and joints, nosing through the snow crust for something to eat.

No wonder the boy was frightened of her. She settles herself on the bed facing him and spreads the quilt over her legs.

"Jesse, did you say? Where were you headed, before you fetched up here?"

"Out California way."

"You have family there?"

"No. Just somewhere to go."

He gets to his feet then and comes toward her, startling her, and she has the gun up before he has taken two steps. He stops and reaches into his pocket with a shaking hand.

"A letter came for you. I forgot about it until just now."

"I'm sorry," she says. She sets the gun on the bed. "Would you read it to me?"

The boy nods. He crouches by the fire, opens the letter, and begins to read, haltingly and without emotion, as if each word were a separate task to him.

"Dear Sadie, I hope you have been well and that the autumn has not been too hard for you. I have come much farther east than I intended and I am writing from . . . Pock—Pog—I don't know."

"Just go on."

"Where my father has been living these many years. He is a merchant now."

The boy stops speaking, but he looks closely at the paper and whispers the words to himself as he reads on.

"Skip the ones you don't know," Sadie says. "When does he say he is coming back?"

The boy folds the letter up. "I oughtn't to read this."

"Read it. I can't read." He looks at the gun on the bed and she places it on the floor, pushing it beneath the bed frame. "All right? Read."

He exhales heavily and begins to read again. "He is a merchant now and has offered me a place on one of his ships that will go through the south seas to take shipments of sugar. I know it is hard of me to leave you but truly the excitement of seeing such places is more than I can bear. I cannot say how many years I will be away and will not ask you to wait for me to come back. You will find a new husband quickly I am sure and you may feel free to never mention me or our marriage. I am sorry again and wish—"

"That's enough," she says. "Stop there."

The boy puts the letter on the floor and sits looking at his stocking feet. "I'm sorry. I didn't know what it was."

"'Course you didn't," she says. Zachary would have known, though, must have known that someone would have to read it to her, that his message would not reach her alone. She pulls the quilt up to her neck and lies very still in the bed. She feels like something is crushing all the breath from her chest. Outside it is almost dark and the wind is picking up. For her, the whole world might be empty except for this one little house. At last she says, "You have a horse, don't you? In the stall out back."

"I do."

"I'll make you a deal, Jesse. You let me use that horse tomorrow to ride to the trading post and get some supplies.

And you help me carry them to a place a little ways out into the prairie. And in return you can have this house and everything left in it. Stay here awhile and head on to California in the spring, if you want. Winter's no time for traveling."

"Are you teasing me?" he says.

"Not a bit. That's a fair bargain, isn't it?"

"More than fair."

"And one other thing. You let me sleep in peace tonight."

"Don't even have to say that," he replies sulkily. "I'm not that kind of man."

"I didn't know it was a kind." She hauls the gun back up from the floor into the crook of her arm and lets the black exhaustion that has been tugging at her pull her under.

She is back in the cave, at the edge of that dark chasm where she saw the blue lights dance, and she holds in her hand a rope that is wondrously long and light. She ties one end fast around a rock and tosses the other into the darkness; it drifts down like a falling leaf. She begins to climb down slowly, hand under hand. Her arms are strong and her descent is steady. The deeper she goes, the lighter it becomes, but the light is strange. It is bright white but it does not hurt her eyes, and in fact she can see better than before. The rock wall in front of her is a whole world of facets and grooves, a lacy mapwork of stone. Her own hands are covered in a tracery of lines; her clothes are a collection of small, careful stitches. Below her, faintly, she can hear music and the swell of voices, and the voices multiply until she is sure there must be hundreds of people. She tries to look down but can see only the light growing brighter, the walls beginning to glow white.

Then a man's voice calls to her from below: "Sadie."

He sounds closer than she expected, close enough almost to touch, but, though she continues her descent, she does not find the bottom.

A moment later another voice, a woman's, calls out again, "Sadie!" and then another woman, and a man, and a child. The air grows warm with voices, layered upon one another, bouncing against the rock. Sadie stops climbing and feels the bite of the rope against her hands, the nearness of the rock at her face.

She is not afraid. She will reach them soon.

"I'm coming," she calls, "I'm almost there," and she lets go of the rope to fall into their waiting arms.

GLASS-LUNG

Henrick Van Jorgen fled Denmark when he was sixteen years old, not because of a crime or a debt or a broken heart, but because he was determined to leave behind the endless memory of his homeland and find a place where he could live with abandon. He landed in New York and, after several years of carousing, consented to marry a solid-looking Danish woman who did not ask too many questions and cooked excellent *fiskeboller,* only to lose her in childbirth a year later when she bore him a daughter.

Some men would have been unnerved by the responsibilities of raising a little girl alone, but Van Jorgen soon learned that the New World, in addition to having plenty of jobs and whiskey and card games he had never heard of, had an abundance of young widows to whom a handsome man with a sad story and a sweet, gray-eyed baby were ir-resistible. Effie never lacked for babysitters, and Van Jorgen never lacked for a good meal.

By his twenty-seventh birthday, Van Jorgen had migrated westward and was living in Pennsylvania, working in a steel mill. It was the best employment he could have imagined. His days were composed of hefting steel beams and tipping pots of molten metal into open-hearth furnaces. He loved the roaring of the mills and the constant glow of the fires that had replaced sunlight in his world. If the work was tough it was also simple and dependable, and he relished the feel of his body functioning as smoothly as any of the machines he used, muscle and bone working together like pistons, making the steel beams that would build the castles of the modern world. He spent his Saturday nights putting those same muscles to work boxing at the athletic club, where he pummeled an assortment of challengers as men in suits gobbled steak, drank porter, and watched him spatter blood on the canvas floor of the ring. At the end of each night he was given two dollars, which he always took home and put directly into a powdered milk tin that he kept under his floorboards.

Effie, his daughter, spent her days in the care of a woman named Mrs. Graf, whose own children had died of Russian flu several years earlier, along with her husband. From the ages of two to eight, Effie learned the skills Mrs. Graf con-sidered most essential, namely how to scrub floors and wash

shirts, which was how she earned her own living. But as
Effie did these things, or even while she ran through the
tenement alleys with the other children, she was always
thinking ahead to the hour when her father would come up
the steps to Mrs. Graf's apartment, clapping his hands and
calling Effie's name from two flights down, smelling of
Biechele's Banner soap and spotted here and there with
traces of soot that he had not managed to wash away in the
basement shower. He would throw open the door without
knocking, sweep her from her feet, and shake her all around
like a squirming puppy. When she had finished laughing, he
would set her down and pass the time with Mrs. Graf for a
few minutes, asking her how the day had gone and whether
his daughter wasn't a perfect angel. Mrs. Graf would hand
him a dish with whatever she had prepared for supper, and
he would set his hands on her shoulders and thank her in a
way that never failed to make her blush. Then he would
take the dish in one hand and lay the other on Effie's head
like a heavy hat, and they would go back to their apartment
and eat. Afterward, Effie would wash the dishes and sit in
her father's lap, and the two of them would look through the
newspaper to see if they could discern what was going on in
the world from the pictures.

There came a week when the normal pattern of work in the
mill was disrupted because one of the furnaces was being
shut down for alterations. The fires had to be extinguished
days in advance so the furnace would have time to cool.

Production was not often stopped—Mr. Carnegie did not abide it except in cases of absolute necessity—but it was rumored that the great man was experimenting with a new product, the patent for which had been sold to him by a Spanish scientist. The process would fuse steel and glass to create a new material that was as strong as steel at one-quarter the weight.

Van Jorgen and a few others were recruited to make alterations to the furnace, under the direction of a small man in wire spectacles. This man wore a fine suit that was already smeared with slag dust, and gave all his instructions in terse, heavily accented English. More often than not, he carried out his orders himself, impatiently wresting tools from the workers' hands and making his own adjustments. Soon the entire group of men was coated in soot; Van Jorgen and the other mill workers climbed in and out of the mouth of the furnace fetching tools and piping, spitting wads of gray phlegm on the floor. There was something fascinating about stepping inside the beast that any other day would have seared the flesh from their bones before they had the time to scream. They strained to lift the heavy pieces of machinery into place, grunting and swearing.

At six o'clock the shift whistle blew and the rest of the men left, but Van Jorgen remained, curious to see what the scientist would do next. The two men sat side by side on a crate catching their breath, and Van Jorgen took a small tin of snuff from his pocket, which he offered to his companion. They relaxed in silence for a few moments, heads spinning pleasantly, and then the scientist led Van Jorgen toward a large box in the corner of the room. With a conspiratorial air, he drew off a heavy canvas cover. The box was as big as a coffin, with a clear glass lid. The scientist, with some effort, lifted one end, and a wave of smoke appeared within.

"Glass," said the scientist, watching Van Jorgen. He shook the box more forcefully, and the smokelike substance swirled into view again. "Very small, very thin pieces of glass." Van Jorgen, bending to look closer, saw that this was so; what had appeared to be smoke was in fact glass fibers as fine as thistledown and light enough to be disturbed by the slightest motion.

"You are building miracles," said Van Jorgen.

The scientist gave a laugh at once shy and giddy as he set the box down and sunk his hands into the pockets of his soot-encrusted suit. "Yes," he said, "that is me."

The following day the apparatus was completed, and the furnace restarted. Before the doors were shut, the Spanish scientist tested a set of bellows almost as large as he was that pumped the smokelike glass into the furnace. Glittering in the heat, the glass filaments alighted on the melting steel like a cloud of flies. The scientist nodded and motioned some of the men to swing shut the riveted metal door through which they had been watching the steel, and to turn the handwheel that would seal it closed. All around the furnace the workers stood with their hands at their sides, jostling for a better look. Even the shift bosses had given up their posturing authority and gathered to watch.

Van Jorgen balanced his weight on the outer edges of his work boots. He had the sense that if he stood still too long the boots might melt to the floor; the room had surpassed even its usual hellish temperature. He backed away from the furnace and resumed his vigil closer to the door, where the flow of air created a cooling draft.

The scientist constantly checked gauges and thermometers, and eventually began heaving at the bellows. He was sweating, red-faced, but he moved with the single-minded zeal of possession. Soon a high-pitched squealing noise like that of twisting metal pierced the air. The men all looked up, startled, but the equipment appeared to be fine. The scientist checked the valves and took a couple more pumps at the bellows, but the noise only grew louder, and he started to move more frantically.

The shift bosses saw his agitation and began questioning him, all of them at once, their voices an unintelligible squabble. The scientist shouted, words beyond the men's understanding, rummaging through a toolbox and waving his hands at them to warn them back. They understood him all in the same moment, and in that moment the furnace blew apart. The scientist and the box of glass filaments were shattered; bricks and chunks of sizzling metal flew; churning heat filled the room. As Van Jorgen turned to run, the glass cloud hit his skin like a mist of fire, searing him across

his arms and neck, burning a spray of holes through the
back of his shirt until the fabric gave way, and then biting
into his skin. He fell to the floor screaming, with the sensation of hot needles piercing his lungs, still reaching for the
door.

Effie sat by her father's hospital bed for most of the next five
days, waiting for him to wake up. The nurses told her repeatedly that the hospital was no place for a little girl, and
Mrs. Graf, who had a terror of hospitals and could not stay
in one for longer than a few minutes, begged her to wait for
news at home. But Effie only twined her legs around the
legs of the chair she sat in and refused to move. When the
nurses changed her father's bandages, they insisted that she
cover her eyes, but as soon as they turned away she peered
from between her fingers. His back was blistered and raw,
and all the hair from the nape of his neck to the crown of his
head had been singed away; from the front he looked like
the same papa she had always known, and from the back
like a red-skinned, boiling monster. The nurses replaced
the bandages and left to attend to the next patient, and he
lay motionless on his side, his breath hissing weakly from
the corners of his mouth, his eyes unmoving beneath their
lids.

When he finally came to, it was early evening and Effie
was the only one in the room, aside from the other patients.
Her father blinked as though waking from a long dream and
gazed up at her from his bed. As soon as his eyes were open

he looked like himself again, and Effie reached out and put her hand on his face, though she had not touched him since he entered the hospital. "Papa," she said. He drew a breath as if to reply, but winced and clutched at his chest. Effie picked up a small brass bell that the nurses had placed on his bedside table and rang it.

A nurse appeared and took Van Jorgen's pulse. Then she sat in Effie's chair and explained to him, slowly and using a variety of metaphors, that in the explosion he had breathed in atomized glass; that it had coated the insides of his lungs, which now suffered minute cracks with every breath. He was lucky to be alive at all, she said, and if he intended to stay alive he must take shallow, slow breaths—inhaling too deeply would cause his lungs to bleed, and doing this too much over time would slowly suffocate him. If he was careful, and stopped when his lungs began to ache, he would be able to summon enough wind to whisper a few words at a time. Then she stood up, as though that settled the matter, and said she would be back in the morning with the doctor. Effie noticed that she did not repeat what the doctor had said on the first day, when he thought Effie could not hear him—that he was sure her father was beyond the aid of science, and would die.

In the dim silence that followed the nurse's departure, Effie stood with her hand on her father's forehead and looked at him. She bent closer, so that her nose was almost touching his, and said, "Can you hear me?" He nodded, and Effie sank back into her chair.

"Mrs. Graf cried all day yesterday," she said, "and she made me wear a dress that used to be her daughter's and go to a funeral. And she gave me dinner and kept calling me 'poor chick.' But the other children were the poor chicks, because all their papas were dead from the fire and you were only just burned. And she put all our things in a box, and she forgot that I don't like barley soup and she made a whole pot of it, just for me, she said."

Van Jorgen parted his fingers and took between them one of her dark, silky curls.

"I ate it," Effie said, "as much as I could."

She pulled her chair closer and bent almost in half so that she could lay her head beside her father's and feel his thready breath on her cheek. The light outside had faded, leaving only a pale blue square of twilight from the window to show them each other's faces, but she could see that his eyes were still open, and he let his hand rest on her head. Inside a minute, she was asleep.

It was four months before Van Jorgen could leave the hospital. He clutched Effie's hand as he walked through the atrium and into the world again; in his other hand he held a small valise with her clothes. The muscles that had once stretched Van Jorgen's skin taut had slackened and wasted during his time in the hospital; even walking without leaning on his daughter's shoulder was an effort. When they reached the street he stopped at the edge of the curb, unable to take the next step. Unsuspected threats seemed to fill every shadow and rut in the road. Effie stepped into the street, pulling him behind her.

They returned to their tenement to find that it had been given to someone else, the mill bosses having assumed Van Jorgen would die. The new man gaped at him as though he were indeed a ghost. Van Jorgen took the powdered milk tin full of his savings from under the floorboard, said his good-byes to Mrs. Graf, and departed.

They went to Philadelphia, where a distant cousin of Van Jorgen's had set up a boardinghouse, and took a set of rooms on the top floor of her building. For a while they lived off of Van Jorgen's savings. He searched for employment but found himself unable to work, a useless man, almost unable to move. He spent hours at night standing before the mirror after Effie went to sleep, holding a candle at his shoulder and craning his neck to look at the mottled red-and-white skin on his back. He wondered if his lungs looked the same; he imagined them hanging like clouds in his chest, swollen with glass instead of rain.

At last he found a job as an assistant to a tailor who was willing to train him. It was slow, boring work, hemming the pants and suit cuffs of the city's wealthy citizens, but it did not require speaking or hard labor, and Van Jorgen learned it quickly. He took the energy that had once been put into the muscle of his work and transformed it into care and precision, for now he was a man whose every breath had to be taken with prudence.

The income he earned from this work slowed the depletion of his hoarded money, but could not stop it. In another two years, the savings were gone. Effie's clothes were shabby and faded, but, despite their poverty, she thrived in her new home. Greta, the cousin in whose building they lived, had taken it upon herself to teach the girl to read and write, and soon Effie brought home stacks of borrowed books, always shuttling them quickly to her bedroom, where she read them by candlelight. Van Jorgen wondered what she was reading and once, when she was off at the market, stole into her room and tried to decipher the stamped titles on the bindings, as if he could intuit from the shape and arrangement of the letters their meaning. But he was unable to make any sense of them, and, furthermore, had the feeling that he was trespassing, that although Effie would never tell him not to enter her room and look at her books, he should not. He straightened the neat stack on her bedside table and left again, no wiser for his pains, and troubled.

By the time she was thirteen, Effie had the poise of a grown woman. She was never frivolous or petulant, and Van Jorgen assumed it was because she had spent so much of her young life caring for him. The idea disturbed him, but it did not bear thinking on; he knew that without her, he would not be able to survive. Van Jorgen would not go to the shops or even to church without her. On the rare occasions when she was sick or busy, he stayed home.

One evening as he and Effie sat at their dinner table, Van Jorgen noticed that his daughter was quieter than usual, and that her face, rather than its regular contemplative calm, had something guilty in it. She ate too fast and spilled soup on the front of her dress, then jumped up and went into the kitchen to dab at it with a rag. When she returned to the table she was flushed and silent.

"Sick?" Van Jorgen asked. He still spoke only with difficulty, but Effie was used to his terseness and usually understood him perfectly.

"No, Papa, I'm fine."

Van Jorgen chewed carefully and stared down into his bowl. Greta was always telling him that he should take more of an interest in Effie, as if she were not his only interest. "She's a girl," Greta said. "She won't tell you anything if you don't ask her."

"Reading now?" Van Jorgen asked.

"No," said Effie, and Van Jorgen frowned. This was not what he had meant, of course, he had meant *what* was she reading, and if she had not been so distracted she would have known that. The question was too trivial to bear repeating, so he searched for some other topic of conversation.

"Greta," he began.

Effie looked up at him and said, "Aunt Greta says there's a job, at the science and art museum."

Van Jorgen pictured the museum, where they had gone once with Greta. It was a tall, yellow sandstone building in the center of town. Effie had adored the place, stopping to read aloud to him every placard and scrap of information, until Greta told her to leave off or they would never see a tenth of the collection. The museum had made no great impression on him, except as a place filled with imposing echoes.

"Won't take me," said Van Jorgen.

"No, Papa," she said. "Not for you. For me."

Van Jorgen could not have been more surprised had a squirrel or a house cat stood up and told him that it planned to seek a post at the bank. Effie, for all her manners, was still a child. He did not mind if she took in washing or mending to earn some extra money, but what could Greta be thinking, sending her off, alone, to that great stone warehouse? Van Jorgen's hands quivered where they rested against the table on either side of his bowl. There were so many flaws in her proposal, so many thoughts to be voiced, that even if he had had the full power of his lungs he would not have had the breath to list them all. He shook his head. "No."

"It's only a secretary's position, nothing difficult," Effie said.

Her father did not answer, only stared at her. She leaned back, thin shoulder blades pressed flat against her chair, her nose and lips coloring as though she were about to cry. But her eyes stayed dry and steady against his. She had been so seldom defiant in the years since his accident that he was now utterly unnerved by a display that most fathers would have found commonplace.

"I've told them I'll do it. I'll start next week. But I can

still walk with you to the streetcar in the morning, and be home before you are. So you shouldn't worry. It's a very good job, and I'll be good at it, I think."

Van Jorgen drew the slow breath he would need to protest, to say that she would be good at anything she tried but that fathers supported their daughters, not the other way around. But Effie disappeared into the kitchen again before he could speak. He banged his spoon against the table, the nearest he could manage to a bellow of frustration and bemusement, but she did not respond.

The man Effie would work for—an archaeologist named Otto Freyn—had a face filled to bursting with aimless ambition. It puffed his plump cheeks, gave a slight glow to his skin, and forced his fair hair into childish ringlets no matter how short he cut it. His fingers were imbued with a slight tremor that, Effie learned much later, did not abate even when he slept. It would be enough to keep him out of the war and leave his naïve optimism intact. He was twenty, freshly graduated from the university, and eager to outstrip the classmates he had left behind.

When Effie's Aunt Greta shepherded her into his office for the first time, they found him reading a large red leatherbound volume entitled *Ancient Peoples of the Southern Americas*. He did not acknowledge them, and when Greta coughed politely, he held up a single finger to beg their patience and read to the end of the page before carefully setting the book down. The look of scrutiny he directed at

Effie made her feel as though her head were too big for her body. But soon Freyn recovered himself, and smiled, and offered her a dish of dusty chocolates from the corner of his desk.

It quickly became clear to Effie that Dr. Freyn had never had a secretary, and that he was pleased to have the honor conferred on him, even if she was only a girl of thirteen who had never had any proper schooling. He seldom looked directly at her, preferring instead to give dictation while she paced behind him down the musty halls of the museum's storage areas, or while staring off into a corner of the room if she were seated beside his desk. For the initial years of her appointment, they carried out a series of menial tasks: cataloguing old collections, drafting letters of thanks or of pleading to philanthropists, serving as couriers for valuable artifacts on loan from other museums.

At first, Effie was awed by Freyn's knowledge; if she phrased her questions properly his answers might last an hour or more. But she soon came to realize that his intelligence was matched only by his single-mindedness. It was impossible for him to divide his attention. If they were cataloguing stuffed birds, he would pore over volumes of ornithological texts, ransack the storage rooms for every last specimen, and create for Effie long lists of scrawled Latin names to be regurgitated by the typewriter and affixed to identifying cards for the display cases. But ask him, in the midst of this fervor, to explain some aspect of Sumerian architecture and he was at a loss, though they had finished with the Sumerian collection only a month before. While Effie absorbed everything he told her and filed it away as neatly as she did the papers on his desk, Freyn seemed to have no memory; or rather, what memory he had was an overgrown jungle in which Hindu temples and Arthurian chalices and even the beloved Ancient Peoples of the Southern Americas were similarly lost among the luxuriant creepers of his far-flung learning.

In four years, Effie cultivated a working knowledge of several sciences and mastered the typewriter. In this time Freyn's stature as an archaeologist increased incrementally, but it was more through the torpid crawl of obligation than any great respect on the part of his colleagues. He published an occasional article in minor journals, suffused with garbled brilliance, but had nothing he could claim as his life's work. His ambition expressed itself most often now as a fevered brightness gleaming from the depths of his eyes.

"Why don't you write a book?" Effie asked him. "Or some lectures?"

"What about?"

"Anything. Mesopotamian pottery."

"Done. Charles Holcomb, *Clay Work in the Fertile Crescent.*"

"Zunis, then. What about those sculptures that were so interesting?"

"Whitfield, done, *Zuni Prayer Totems, Their Uses and Construction.* Only two years ago."

"Well, really."

"I want something that's mine."

"You won't find it in someone else's book," Effie said, looking pointedly at the stack of thick volumes on his desk, newly arrived from the library. "You'd do better to check the storage halls."

"Do you think?" he said, staring at her suddenly in a way that left her flustered and hot-faced, the kind of look she had previously seen him lavish only on antiquities.

"What?" she asked. "I don't know. It couldn't hurt."

Freyn reached out toward her, as though he might brush back one of the strands of loose hair that lay across her forehead, or place his hand on her cheek, but just as abruptly, he pulled his hand back and slipped it into his pocket, looked down at the floor and shook his head. "You're right, I'm sure," he said. "Very astute of you."

The next day they began to explore the dark recesses of the storage halls, moving through the grimy rooms as though the museum's basement was their own private country, a dusky, bereft world that smelled of excelsior and naphthalene. The keen glass eyes of stuffed rodents observed them from forgotten display cases as Freyn and Effie squeezed between old packing crates. The thrill of exploration consumed them both, although Freyn turned his enthusiasm indiscriminately to everything they saw, while Effie dismissed most of their finds after a few minutes. After several weeks of searching, they discovered an Egyptian collection that, according to the packing slip, had been shipped to the museum more than twenty years before but had never been

uncrated. Attached to the slip was a letter written in a cor-
dial, wavering hand from an old professor in Vermont, thank-
ing the curator for giving a good home to the collection it
had taken him a lifetime to accumulate.

Throughout the winter the Egyptian artifacts absorbed
all of Freyn and Effie's attention. Their workdays grew longer and longer, and it was often past suppertime when Effie
arrived home in her dust-streaked dress. Sometimes she
felt a stab of guilt when she saw the look of distress on her
father's face as she walked through the door hours late, a
guilt that only deepened at the way he turned aside and
quickly composed himself before he welcomed her home.
But the draw of the museum was irresistible, and when she
and Freyn were in its grip everything else was crowded to
the back of her mind.

It all came to an end one morning when Effie arrived at
the office to find Freyn thoroughly drunk, waving a large
sheet of paper covered in his scrawling handwriting. Trans-
lating various arcane works from the Egyptian collection, he
told her, combining information from several hieroglyphic
inscriptions, triangulating a location with the oases at Siwa
and Farafra, he had pieced together a map of a burial site in
Egypt that he felt confident would yield treasure unlike
anything the museums of the world yet possessed.

He offered her a glass of brandy in celebration, which
she refused, and soon fell asleep at his desk. Gently, Effie
withdrew Freyn's notes from under his cheek, and picked
her way through his tangled chain of thought. Every link

was strong. Excitement bloomed in her chest, like a crocus unfurling from the snow.

The next several months were a flurry of secretive activity as Effie and Freyn attempted to plan an excavation in Egypt without letting anyone know what exactly he hoped to find. If his supervisors at the museum discovered his intention, they would surely send someone else. Worse yet, if the British or the Germans were somehow to find out about it, they would have their own teams in Egypt hauling the grave site over before he had even set out. Everything, from raising money to hiring assistants, had to be done with the utmost artifice, and in this, Effie was indispensable. She had a way of convincing people to be helpful without them feeling that it had been her idea, and soon Freyn had a sizeable budget and two dozen steamer trunks' worth of supplies.

As much as Effie appreciated her professional relationship with Dr. Freyn, she could not help imagining, from time to time, that he might someday see her as more than a secretary. It was true that he sometimes took her hand as they discussed the best strategies for his upcoming trip, but he did so with the same distracted air with which he handled his paperweights and pens. He listened to her ideas with enthusiasm, but she had no reason to believe it was any different from the enthusiasm he lavished on mummified cats and rusted iron figurines. And why should it be? She was his subordinate, after all, and when she thought about it she realized that she knew almost nothing about what he did outside his office. In addition, he was leaving for Egypt in two months, and might be gone for years. And of course there was her father to consider; it was only pride and selfishness that made her entertain such thoughts.

Nonetheless, the idea continued to plague her, but nothing in Freyn's words or manner gave her any particular hope until one day, as she was preparing to leave, he grabbed hold of her hand and said, "Miss Van Jorgen, I wonder if you will join me for supper tomorrow at my house?"

Effie caught her breath and stood speechless for a moment, torn between the desire to accept immediately and the impropriety of what he had proposed; of course she could not visit him alone.

Freyn blinked back at her for several long seconds before the puzzled expression cleared from his face. "Ah," he said. "And of course your father must come, too. You live with him, don't you?"

"Yes," said Effie quietly, believing that she would never convince her father to go, but overcome with curiosity about Dr. Freyn's home. She imagined it would be messy; he always left papers and odds and ends around the office. *But he will have a housekeeper,* she told herself, *and a cook, and who knows, maybe a valet, too. If I were to live there, what would I do with myself all day?* She blushed, embarrassed by her own daydreaming, and said she would give him an answer the following morning.

•••

Effie repeated the invitation to her father, unaware of how the corners of her mouth twitched up in a shy smile whenever she said Freyn's name. As she went on to describe the voyage Dr. Freyn would soon be undertaking, the genius of his discovery, and the fame that would undoubtedly be his, Van Jorgen noted her exhilaration with growing dismay. At last, he stopped her with a wave of his hand and said that they would go. He could tell she was surprised, but she only nodded, picked up a basket, and left to buy the groceries for their supper. Van Jorgen sat in an armchair in front of a window that had a view onto the street below. He saw Effie emerge from the building, and step lightly across the cobblestones toward the market.

She was not a girl anymore. He had known, of course, that someday she would fall in love, be married, and leave him, but he saw now that he had never really let himself believe it. If he had been a different man, the man he should have been, her suitors would have come to him first, looked at him with fear and respect and courted his favor as well as Effie's. Instead they invited her to supper without even showing him their faces. He was not a man now, not even a father; he was only a cripple. His daughter would make sure he was provided for, of course, hire some garrulous matron to wash his clothes and wheel him to church in a chair while Effie attended to the needs of her own household. But the heart of it was that she would marry and go. He longed, for the first time, for Denmark, for a place where old men were propped up at the supper table, fed soup, and cared for even when they were beyond use.

The pall of dusk had settled over the streets, and the people walked more hurriedly. Effie would be darting from the baker to the grocer, accumulating vegetables and bread and maybe some cuts of meat, the basket growing heavier on her sturdy arm, a ready smile for everyone she met. He should be with her, to protect her in the gathering dark, but he was no help to anyone. He could not even buy her a wedding dress in which to leave him.

The following night, Van Jorgen and Effie arrived at Freyn's house just as the lamps came on, Van Jorgen leaning on his daughter's arm. He was wearing his Sunday shirt, and Effie had a length of satin ribbon in her hair that Van Jorgen had presented to her as she was getting ready for the evening. He saw now that it was a different shade of green than her dress, but she had thanked him with tears in her eyes all the same, and kissed his rough cheek.

The housekeeper greeted them at the door, but Freyn, unable to control his eagerness, stood just behind her, looking over her shoulder. Van Jorgen saw the face of his enemy and was disarmed by its childishness. He had pictured a man who was slick and handsome, pompously dressed, but Freyn's collar stud had come undone, he was sweating, and his smile was exuberant and fawning.

"Very good to meet you, sir," he said, and shook Van Jorgen's hand.

"Papa doesn't speak much, on account of his health," said Effie.

Freyn smiled and nodded. "Maybe we should sit down?" His eyes moved back and forth between Effie and Van Jorgen, as though he were not sure whom he was asking.

They moved to the drawing room. Effie and Freyn chatted comfortably, starting out with talk about work but then moving on to politics, the war, and finally to things of no consequence that made for more pleasant conversation. Once in a while Freyn would remember himself and direct a question at Van Jorgen. Van Jorgen would gather his breath and issue a terse reply, and soon the conversation would drift away from him again. It did not matter. He did not care what they were saying. What was more important was the way they looked at each other, sat so comfortably close, the easy way that Effie laughed. He had not heard her laugh so much since she was a child, perhaps not even then. She was flushed and glowing before him, her infatuation all too clear.

Van Jorgen stood abruptly and moved away from the two young people. Freyn did not notice, and chose that moment to grasp Effie's hand and begin describing in detail the difficulty of finding reliable workers in Egypt.

Van Jorgen went into the next room, a modest-sized library with a table, chair, and reading lamp at its center. Beneath each of the several windows was a case of specimens, collections from Freyn's studies over the years. Most of them were unremarkable objects: shells, pottery shards, a few glass bangles that were over a thousand years old but the like of which could be found in the collection of any antiquities enthusiast anywhere. Another case held rock and mineral specimens: a great bubbling chunk of malachite, a polished orb of rose quartz, some others that were not labeled.

In one corner of this case was a piece that looked like a tree branch made of stone. The main trunk of it was as thick as a carrot and about a foot long, with three short auxiliary branches at one end. It sparkled even in the dim light of the library. Van Jorgen felt a pain in his chest and realized that his heart was racing, that he was breathing too quickly, and he forced himself to slow down.

He tested the top of the case and found it unlocked. Back in the drawing room he could hear Freyn and his daughter still locked in rapt conversation. Lifting the glass, he touched the strange object. He had expected a shock of some sort, but felt only a curious fluid roughness, as though the rock sighed at his touch. He closed his eyes and walked his fingertips along the length of the branched object, exploring each dip and turn in its structure.

"Papa!" said Effie. "You mustn't touch those things."

She was at his side, taking hold of his arm, but Van Jorgen did not move his fingers. Freyn approached and Van Jorgen looked up, feeling like a dog who has been caught with some prized scrap of offal and knows it is about to be stolen. Freyn smiled at him and patted Effie's shoulder.

"I see you've found the fulgurite, sir. A very rare specimen purchased at a market in Egypt, during my student days. The Bedouins sometimes discover them in the desert after a windstorm. This," he said, indicating a small hole at one end, "is where a bolt of lightning struck the sand, and all around it the sand fused into glass."

Effie made another flustered appeal to her father to release the fulgurite, but Van Jorgen was barely listening. All he could think was that the insides of his own maimed lungs must look something like this: crystalline, brittle. He lifted the fulgurite with the utmost care and cradled it in his palms. Freyn seemed to have forgotten the fulgurite entirely. He was shifting his weight back and forth between his feet, and gazing at the ceiling with a rapturous look.

"Do you know," he said, "you should come with me to Egypt when I go next month. Both of you," he said, in breathless excitement, glancing at Effie's stunned face but charging on nonetheless. "I need her there as my assistant, and I'm sure she would not consent to go without you. As a chaperone, that is. And surely you would enjoy seeing the country, sir."

Van Jorgen frowned. He was loath to accept anything from the man who was going to steal his daughter, worse yet such an expensive gift. He was not taken in for a moment by talk of a chaperone. While propriety certainly required it, a fitter person could be found to accompany Effie. But he looked at the fulgurite and was enchanted. The thought of going to Egypt, the place that produced such marvels, had a heady appeal that subsumed even his pride. He imagined within the desert a forest of fulgurites, their branched arms reaching toward the sky, beckoning the lightning down like a multitude of snakes beseeching their charmer. When he left Freyn's house that night, the fulgurite, wrapped in silk pillowcases and carefully placed in a crate, was with him.

The next month was a flurry of plans and packing. Freyn booked their passage for the two-week journey to Alexandria. He went to town with Effie and Greta to purchase the clothes Effie would need—sturdy boots and light cotton skirts, only a single layer over pantaloons. It was all packed into trunks, labeled and strapped and carried off to the shipping yard.

Van Jorgen eschewed such mundane tasks, waved away Freyn's offer to buy him a new suit, and did not leave the house until the day of their departure, when he, Effie, and Freyn rode together to the dock. In that time he built a box for the fulgurite, velvet-lined, made of oak, and once he had packed his treasure into it he refused to relinquish it.

The sea journey was long but uneventful. They arrived in Alexandria at night, and set out the next morning for the oasis at Siwa. There they collected workers and supplies, and began the arduous journey toward the dig site, a week's trek through empty desert, traveling in a caravan. Freyn kept his map close, guarded jealously and consulted often, though it was unlikely that anyone would follow them. Most archaeologists believed that even the Valley of the Kings was exhausted at this point, and the Western Desert—well, it was a wasteland, impossible that anything of worth would be uncovered there. And yet Freyn was convinced otherwise. He stopped to take measurements and make calculations, and finally they found their camp.

The spot Freyn indicated looked to Effie no different from any of the land they had passed through; there was nothing but sand in every direction, rolling dunes that were fiercely golden in the day, then purple and gray in the evening. As soon as the party had pitched their tents, clustered around the six great water tanks that had made up the bulk of their freight, Freyn sent a small group of workers back toward Siwa for more water, a process that would have to be repeated every few days for as long as they remained in the desert.

The environment was as inhospitable as one could imagine—desiccated, mercilessly hot, and scoured over by sand-bearing winds—but Effie loved it. During their first nights in camp she would creep away from the tents while everyone else slept, and sit looking out at the horizon, where the hunched backs of the sand dunes rose up against the thickly sewn stars. Her father, too, flourished in the desert. During the day the hot air seemed to soften his glassed lungs, to render them slightly more pliant, and his breathing easier, and though he was still only a shadow of the man she remembered from her childhood, it was heartening to see him walking around the camp without stopping every few paces to catch his breath.

The diggers began their work. Even with Freyn's map, the location was not precise, and they had several hundred empty hectares of sand to investigate. The men set to work with shovels, loading the sand into boxes and dragging it aside. For the first few days, Effie sat in her stifling tent and listened to their grunts and clangings, to the songs they sang to keep themselves going. They worked from before sunup until ten o'clock in the morning, when the heat became too intense to tolerate and they retreated to the tents. They ate their lunch and slept, and took up their work again at five o'clock, working until eleven by the light of kerosene lamps. But Effie's curiosity would not allow her to sit aside for long, and soon she was outside in even the fiercest heat, standing with Freyn as he searched again through the notes she had taken from the collection, hoping to find some new information. They had left their old roles at home, and instead of treating her like a secretary he now spoke to her as a dear and trusted companion, seeking her opinion on his smallest decisions, even arguing with her on occasion in full confidence that she would consider his points and argue back.

But months passed without any sign of a find. Every few days a team of camel drivers returned with more barrels of water; every two weeks they brought food. Freyn made sure the diggers were well fed and well paid, but it did not mollify them. Curses replaced singing as their daily accompaniment. Effie did not have to speak their language to know what they said about Freyn: that he was mad, their work pointless. The strain showed in Freyn's face each afternoon as they sat down for lunch, worry that he would be thought a fool, that he would lose his post at the museum, that he would have to go home without a return on his investors' backing. The sun had bleached his fair hair white, turned his face and neck a livid pink, and after a year in the desert he had developed a nervous habit of running his hands frequently across his face to brush away traces of sand, all of which made him look slightly crazed. Effie still believed in his genius as surely as she had that first day in his office, but she wondered sometimes if his intellect might outrun his strength.

As they entered their second year at the dig site, the sun grew fiercer. Work had to be stopped by nine and could not be resumed until sunset. In the intense heat Van Jorgen was freed of the lethargy that overtook the rest of the party, feeling instead a vitality as shimmering as the air that hovered over the sand. He was able to walk long distances for the first time in years, and was glad to be free of the camp, where Freyn's prattling irritated him and Effie's doting affection for the man troubled his heart. Saddled with oiled leather bags of water, Van Jorgen roamed the dunes in the hottest hours of the day, flouting sun-sickness and the disorienting mutability of the desert landscape. There were no cacti, no rocks, only hills and gullies and curves of sand that changed daily. After Effie had failed to dissuade him from these ramblings, she convinced Freyn to erect a flagpole with a red flag, so that her father might have some landmark by which to find his way home.

Van Jorgen liked the exercise, the feeling of his limbs moving again as limbs ought to. The walks were difficult, his feet sinking into the sand, but he cherished the burning of muscles that had been dormant for years. He had long since abandoned the clothes he arrived in and had started dressing like a Bedouin, wearing long cotton tunics and head wraps that allowed the desert heat to flow off of him, and he had taken to carrying the fulgurite with him. Far from the camp, he took it from its box and held it as he walked. Now and then he felt a twinge in his fingers, and with it a slight earthward twitch of the fulgurite. At times he spoke to it, softly and soothingly, as though it were a favored pet or a fretful child. He walked as long as he could, until evening came on and the heat of the desert began to fade, leaving him breathless and pained.

At night he lay awake in his canvas tent, sometimes for hours, listening to the wind beat against the tent flaps and watching it bulge the walls. The fulgurite rested on his chest, rising and lowering with the motion of his breath, and he ran his fingers over its whorls and depressions, along the three short branches, across the opening that had, for one-millionth of a second, held a bolt of lightning.

One day Van Jorgen returned to camp at sunset and noticed that there was no one at the excavation pit. The workers were sitting cross-legged outside their tents, talking in low voices with great intensity. He went to Freyn's tent, heard Freyn and Effie speaking inside, and instead of entering stood still, listening. He could see the two of them faintly through a gap in the canvas walls of the tent, Freyn sitting on his bed with his head in his hands, Effie at his side, trying her best to soothe him. Even with her sunburned face, her grave expression, Van Jorgen was struck by how handsome she was. He could barely recall her mother's face, so much time having passed since her death, and so little in their marriage. Effie had such vibrancy, such beauty and self-possession, that he could not believe she was his child. *She isn't*, he thought. *She's the child of a man who died in a steel mill back before the start of the war. And see how she flourishes*. He had watched her beside Freyn, beside the workers at the excavation pit, shovel in hand, digging with them on the worst days, giving whatever strength she had not because one more pair of hands made much difference, but because her belief could stand in for Freyn's when it faltered. She turned to Freyn now, took his hands in hers, and kissed them.

"I tried to offer the workers credit," Freyn said. "A share of the find. There's no more money."

"We'll find something. I'll go back to Alexandria if I have to, send some telegrams home."

Freyn breathed slowly, his eyes squeezed shut as though he were afraid to open them. "It's pointless," he said. "Who would back me now? We'll have to leave in a month, if not before."

Van Jorgen turned away, closing his own eyes, their voices still filtering to him through the tent walls. He could see what would happen from here. Freyn would be disgraced, impoverished, a laughingstock; he might become unhinged. Effie would try her best to help him, but he would succumb to such depression that eventually, at her father's gentle coaxing, she would abandon him. And then she would be free again, free to care for Van Jorgen for as long as he could maintain his tenuous place in the world of the living. It shamed him to take such joy in the prospect— and yet, he asked himself, was she not better off under his care than wedded to a madman?

The next day Van Jorgen woke early, before the blush of light colored the night sky. The workers had not even emerged from their tents, and the air was still cold and clear, but he was overcome with restlessness and could not bring himself to sit still, much less sleep. He took the fulgurite and his water bags, and started slowly into the desert.

In the past he had always kept track of the camp's location, but now he cleared his mind entirely and walked without thinking, basking in the growing light and heat, until he saw that the sky was being quenched by inky clouds. In the two years they had been in the desert, what little rain they had seen had been intense but momentary; the thunderheads above seemed to portend a larger storm. Soon the horizon was strewn with forks of lightning, strobing silver light scattering across the sand. There was no rain yet, but the wind had picked up, spraying him with grit. He wrapped the end of his turban around his face, rendering himself blind but shielding his eyes from the sand, and continued walking.

Van Jorgen moved toward the lightning, until he believed he could feel the heat shift minutely with each flash. The air all around him was charged; if he were to draw his finger along the sand he thought it might light like a match. The fulgurite felt alive in his hands; at times it nearly jerked him off his feet with its eagerness to move forward. The surface of the glass seemed to crawl and shudder a few seconds after each flash of lightning, as though the lightning and the glass were engaged in a call-and-response. The white light of the flashes cut through his cotton shroud into his eyes. He was breathing quickly, panting. Beneath his feet the sand felt as though it had softened into flour; it was almost impossible not to stumble, but the fulgurite tugged him along. Then, suddenly, it stopped. It still quivered with energy, but it did not pull him. Van Jorgen turned a slow circle, arms stretched to their limits to urge the fulgurite onward, but it did not move. Its surface sang with electricity, and the lightning seemed to be flashing around him now instead of ahead of him, all the glory of the heavens coursing earthward in short bursts. He turned in a circle, twice, three times, sinking to the ankles in cool, restless sand.

Setting the fulgurite carefully on the ground before him, Van Jorgen got to his knees. *Without eyes and without a voice, what do I have left?* he thought. He plunged his hands into the sand as though he were sitting atop a great stream. The rain began to fall. The first drops evaporated in midair, virga drunk by the parched atmosphere, but soon thick, warm gobbets of water pelted his back. Van Jorgen dug with his fingers into sand that was soaked for the first time in years, until the hole he had created held his whole torso. He sifted the sand through his fingers, rubbed the grains of it across his palms, but he found nothing. As he worked the storm dissipated, until the sun shone harshly on him again, and he became aware of a voice faintly calling his name. He unwound the turban from his eyes, and a moment later, Freyn appeared over the edge of a nearby dune. He ran to Van Jorgen's side and sat down heavily in the sand. Van Jorgen handed him one of the water bags, and Freyn drank.

"Effie was worried about you, with the storm," he said. "In tears, if you can believe it. I told her I would look for you."

Van Jorgen nodded, keenly aware of the hole in the sand, the fulgurite, wondering when Freyn would notice either, how he could explain them. He pressed his dry tongue against the roof of his mouth. The easiest distraction would be to mention the imminent failure of the expedition. There were plenty of reasons he could present to Freyn for leaving immediately, reasons that could be cloaked as concern for Effie and himself. Other explorers had searched for much longer, it was true, but not under such conditions, a hundred miles from the nearest source of water. One day something would go wrong; the water bearers would not come, there would be a sandstorm too intense, and then the desert would swallow them all. Better to give up. Better for Freyn to salvage what was left of his reputation and go home.

Freyn had meshed his fingers together and sat looking at them where they rested in his lap. His hands trembled, and Van Jorgen could see that a blister had torn loose from Freyn's thumb, leaving a large, raw wound there.

"She never cries, does she?" said Freyn. "I'm sure I have never seen her cry before. Even though . . . well. I've failed her, and so you, too. Two years I've tortured all of us in this place, and for nothing. How foolish, to think life could go on like this."

Van Jorgen turned his gaze back to the sand at his feet, but his mind was not so easily cleared. The look of despair on Freyn's face was not unfamiliar to him. Freyn had clearly believed with all his heart that whatever dream he saved himself for all these years, like a virgin bride, would reward him by promptly coming true. The younger man could be Van Jorgen years back, living in blissful ignorance of the pain of the world, only to have it pour over him in a molten wave. Van Jorgen found himself wishing viciously that Freyn would begin to weep, so that there would be some proof that he was weak, unworthy of the treasure he sought. But when he looked up again and caught Freyn's gaze, the young man only laughed bitterly and handed Van Jorgen a fistful of sand.

"There you are," he said. "We can take it back to America and tell everyone it's the Sand of the Pharaohs. Auction it off to some other poor dunce waiting to be sold a fantasy."

Van Jorgen sifted the sand back and forth between his cupped hands, nodded toward the hole he had dug and mustered a breath. "I thought. There was. Something. Here."

Freyn looked behind them at the pit in the sand. "Here? Why here?"

Van Jorgen gestured vaguely to the fulgurite and shrugged. He wasn't sure whether he would have been able to explain himself even without his handicap, but he could see that Freyn was intrigued, already poking his hand into the hole as though it would exude some palpable marker of success. Van Jorgen crawled over and knelt beside him. He drew a long, slow breath and spoke in a whisper so quiet it was almost inaudible. "Maybe fortune smiles on *us* for once."

It would take another two weeks to move the camp to the spot the fulgurite had indicated, cajole the workers into one last attempt, follow Van Jorgen's inexorable instructions to go down, farther down, until at last one shovel struck against the stone shell of a tomb, and the workers fell silent. Another three months would be spent in careful excavation— boxes of sand carted away, reinforcements built, armed mercenaries hired to protect the site—before the entrance to the burial chamber was opened, the richly hieroglyphed walls exposed to the light of the torch, the false burial chamber discovered, and then the true one. Inside was a tomb the like of which was not to be found in any museum anywhere: an entire room studded with beads and cabochons of pale green glass, purer than the windows of any church on the Continent, that glowed in the unaccustomed light like fireflies. In the center of the room was a sarcophagus likewise adorned, the smiling pharaoh clasping against his chest a scarab the size of a human heart, carved out of that same flawless green.

In a month, the mercenaries would have their hands full fighting off grave robbers; in two, Freyn would be engaged in disputes with the Egyptian government; in five months, Carter's discovery of Tutankhamen's tomb, with its ostentatious gilding and hoards of jewelry, would nudge their elegant, green treasure chamber into comparative obscurity. But as Freyn and Effie and Van Jorgen cracked open the entrance to the crypt, all they could imagine was the glory that had so long eluded them. Freyn stepped back and nodded to Van Jorgen, but Van Jorgen grasped his hand, and Effie's, and walked with them into the shining glass vault, amid treasure that had slept through the birth and death of a hundred generations.

LOGGING LAKE

Robert checked his watch for what had to have been the dozenth time. It was only two o'clock in the afternoon, and already it felt like one of the longest days of his life. He and Terri had left Seattle on a predawn flight and arrived at Glacier National Park several hours later, where they spent some time buying last-minute supplies at the only store open this early in the season. Terri had enticed Robert on this trip with tales of her hiking prowess and the glory of unspoiled nature, but now that they were here he was beginning to wonder if she had ever done more than jog through Discovery Park. Lots of things seemed to surprise her: the snow on the ground in May; the fact that you needed a permit to camp; the signs that advised against drinking from the rivers, though the glacier meltwater was icy blue and so clear you could count the rocks at the bottom of the riverbed. But, he reminded himself, those were the kinds of things Old Bob would worry about. He was New Bob, or rather New Robert, and New Robert's motto was *Say Yes to Everything*.

He went to stand beside Terri, who was bent over a park map, nodding her head seriously as a ranger drew his finger along various possible routes.

"What sort of difficulty level are you looking for?" the ranger asked.

"Difficult," said Terri.

"Or medium. Or easy, maybe," Robert said, though it hurt his pride to do it. He had forgotten what a drag dating was, the constant posturing and wondering how the other person would judge your every action. Still, it would only be worse if he ended up in over his head, struggling red-faced up some craggy incline while Terri bounded ahead of him like a mountain goat.

The ranger looked out the window. "This late in the day, I think your best bet is the trail to Grace Lake," he said. He tapped a dotted line that snaked up a long road and into a dense green patch on the map.

"Great," said Terri. "Can we take this map?"

"This?" the ranger said. "I mean, this won't really do you any good. You need a topo map. Number 18, I think."

"Yeah, I love the topos," Terri said, giving Robert a wink that was perhaps meant to be reassuring but came across as lascivious, and he smiled back uneasily. The more time he

spent with Terri the more he was convinced she was constantly sending him signals he didn't know how to interpret.
Or maybe it was just women in general that he couldn't
read.

Bob had spent most of his adult life dating a woman named
Linda, eight years that stretched from the end of graduate
school until the previous summer. He had initially been at-
tracted to her because of the effortless sensibleness with
which she ordered and commanded her life. That is, until
the day she came home and suggested they move to Paris.

"But why would we do that?" he said.

"Why not?"

"Well, we don't speak French. And I don't think we can
even work there, legally. Plus, I like my job here."

"You *like* industrial chemistry?"

Bob eyed her warily. Linda knew he enjoyed his work,
but this was not his frank, dependable Linda. This was some
wild-eyed stranger. He suspected her friend Preeta was to
blame. Preeta shared a desk with Linda at work, and she
was single and a bit flighty. She occasionally got large cash
gifts from her childless aunts and uncles, which she spent
on everything from spa trips to Iceland to having long, wavy
Arabian horse mane extensions woven into her hair. Usually
Linda would come home and tell Bob about these exploits
with arch glee, and the two of them would laugh together.
But, once in a while, Preeta managed to convince Linda
that one of her affectations was an unmissable opportunity.

Linda laid a brochure on the table: MASSAGE THERAPY
IN PARIS! The photograph showed a sunny room and a
woman kneading the back of a blissful, towel-wrapped man.

"You want to massage people?"

"Do you have to be so literal about everything?" she said,
throwing her purse on the couch. "It doesn't have to be that.
It doesn't even have to be Paris. But don't you get tired of
everything being the same all the time? Preeta says—"

"Ha!" said Bob, little more than an exhalation of excitement, but he knew immediately that it was a mistake.

"What does *that* mean?" Linda asked.

"It means it's another one of Preeta's crazy ideas that
she's managed to pass along to you."

"Is it so crazy to think we might do something fun and
romantic for once? Are we going to stay holed up here like
scared animals for the rest of our lives, eating Fig Newtons
and watching the Discovery Channel every night?"

Bob flinched. He loved Fig Newtons. And the Discovery
Channel. He'd thought Linda did, too; they had good conversations about the shows.

"The problem with you is you can't even *imagine* it,"
Linda said, brushing away angry tears. "You can't even get
your head around the idea of something different, so you're
just going to say no."

The next morning, with her eyes still pink and a strong
cup of coffee in hand, she delivered a speech he could tell
she'd been practicing in her head all night, if not all year:
She still loved him, but they'd been together too long. They

were stagnating each other, holding each other back; it would be better for them both if they just stopped pretending.

"I'm not pretending anything," Bob said. "What do you want me to do? You want me to move to Paris to prove a point?"

Linda said nothing, just shook her head. She packed up all her belongings from their apartment and was gone within a week.

In the wake of her departure, Bob spent months in a black funk. He volunteered to work sixty-hour weeks, ignored his friends' phone calls, and fell asleep on the couch every night watching TV and eating cereal from the box. Fig Newtons were ruined for him; he could not even bear to look at the package in the grocery store. By the time midwinter hit, he knew he had to do something or risk spending the rest of his thirties lost in a swoon of self-pity. He bought a case of beer and called up a few of his buddies. They spent the night crafting an online dating profile that would usher in his new life. His friend César chose a photo where Bob was staring straight at the camera, smiling and inexplicably gripping a gymnastics trophy, the thinning patch in the back of his hair entirely hidden. César cropped Linda out and applied some filter that made Bob's pasty skin look tanned, and voilà: Bob Lambros was dead, and here was Robert L., the kind of man who didn't take no for an answer.

Except that he had to, repeatedly. His initial night of euphoria gave way to a months-long string of messages to women who never responded, unless it was to tell him to go away. Until Terri reached out to him. Her pictures were sexy but not trashy, and her profile didn't contain any obvious red flags. He could only hope that things were finally turning around.

Terri suggested a new Korean restaurant and Bob arrived early for their date, but she was already there, sitting at a table with an empty water glass. She stood up and said, "Robert!," ignoring the hand he offered in favor of hugging him warmly. He sat down across from her while she flagged down a waiter and said, "Two bottles of soju, please."

"Oh, no thanks."

"You have to try it," she said. "If you hate it, just get something else."

He forced himself to smile, to sip the drink when it was handed to him and nod appreciatively. He hated it. He hated any kind of alcohol other than beer. But that was not the point. The point was to relax and go with the flow.

Within an hour he decided he might be in love with Terri or he might never want to see her again. She was full of brazen energy and was every bit as attractive as her photos made her out to be—lusciously curvy, with a face that flushed with pleasure every time she laughed. She made a point of touching him as she talked, casually resting her hand on his wrist or fingers to emphasize a point. But Terri also had a habit of lapsing into silence and staring at him, and repeatedly quoted from Robert's dating profile, which he now saw he had crafted to sound interesting without thinking much about accuracy. For instance, he had written that he loved nature. As soon as Terri mentioned it, Robert realized he had not clarified *how* he loved nature, which was in a gentle, distant way: He liked flipping through big, glossy coffee-table books with *National Geographic* photos, or stopping to admire a particularly fiery leaf on the sidewalk in fall; he would even sit out on the stoop on occasion just to listen to the birds in the early morning, but he never ventured farther from civilization than that.

When the check arrived Robert handed the waiter his credit card, and while he waited for the receipt, Terri stood up and began putting on her coat.

"You drove, right?" she said. "I'm at Sixty-eighth and Highland. It's a yellow brick high-rise. The lock on the lobby door's broken, so just come up. Number 422."

"Oh. Sure," said Robert. Wasn't he supposed to have to talk her into going back to her place? Or at least ask? She seemed so sure of herself, as if everything had been agreed on ahead of time. But why not? The three sojus he'd drunk had tasted terrible but had gone right to his head; he felt like he could crush a brick with his bare hands. He probably shouldn't be driving, but fuck it.

When Robert arrived at Terri's building there was no elevator that he could see, so he climbed the stairs, winded and sweaty by the time he reached the fourth floor. He knocked at her apartment, got no answer, and, finding the door unlocked, he hesitantly pushed it open. Inside it was so dark that he couldn't make out anything but the hulking shapes of the furniture. There was a strong smell of smoke. For a moment he stood frozen in the doorway. "Terri?" he said.

"In here."

He stepped gingerly across the carpet, groping ahead of him in the darkness, and managed to find the door to her bedroom, fumbling his way inside.

The room was as bright as the rest of the apartment was dark, lit by lamps in every corner and filled with a haze of incense. Terri was sitting cross-legged on her bed, naked, reading a book. Robert inhaled sharply. The lamps made Terri's skin look golden, or maybe it was the alcohol, but she seemed almost too perfect to touch. Terri put the book down and looked at him with that same disconcerting stare she had focused on him in the restaurant. Robert stood gripped by a mixture of lust and intense self-consciousness, painfully aware of his sweaty back and sour breath.

"Well, come on," she said, and that was that. It had been so long since he'd had sex with anyone other than Linda that he was nervous in spite of being drunk, but it didn't matter because Terri made love as though she had something to prove: loud and energetic and dramatic, like they were simultaneously filming a sex scene for the Oscars and engaged in some high-concept contest to see who could have the most fun. And it *was* fun, and cathartic at the same time, and to hell with Linda, there was nothing wrong with him.

...

Afterward, they showered together. Robert stood behind Terri with his arms around her, watching the water pouring over her shoulders and between her breasts, breathing in the warm steam and thinking that for the first time in nearly a year he could actually say he was happy, when she turned to face him and said, "I'm going hiking in Montana in two weeks. Want to come along?"

Robert stuttered. Thanks to all the overtime he'd worked in the past year, he had money and vacation days to spare. But he hated traveling and knew next to nothing about Terri. Still, he knew what New Robert would say. New Robert would *take the bull by the horns* and *seize the day* and *live for the moment* and sign up immediately for a wilderness sexcapade. New Robert would have suggested it himself.

"Hell yes, I do," he said.

They went to bed soon after, but at six o'clock the next morning Robert found himself wide awake and restless. He crawled out of bed and put on his stale clothes from the night before. Terri half woke and looked at him.

"Heading out?" she said.

"I would love to stay longer, it's just—"

"Door locks from the inside," she said, and snuggled deeper into her pillow.

Robert closed the bedroom door behind him and turned to leave. The rest of the apartment, in the gray light of day, looked like it had been ransacked. One wall bore dark splatter stains with dents at their centers and a scattering of shattered glass at its base. Everywhere were drawers torn out and dumped; a small side table held an armless teddy bear and a cluster of candles burned down into a massive pool of wax. The smoky smell from the night before was even stronger.

Suddenly it all made sense. Terri was gorgeous, funny, a great lay, and completely fucking nuts. No wonder she had messaged him. He thanked God she didn't have his phone number and made a beeline for the door. Bullet dodged.

Then he got home and his apartment looked like the depressing hellhole it was—all the gaps in the bookshelves where Linda had taken her books, the empty fridge, and neat rows of cereal boxes in the cupboard. After two days he couldn't stand it anymore. So Terri was a shitty housekeeper, and possibly deranged. So what. Anything was better than this.

But now, *now* that they were trudging toward some godforsaken campsite in the middle of nowhere Montana, he was beginning to have doubts. Especially given that an hour after leaving the ranger station they had made it only two miles up the road. Robert's pack was listing heavily to one side and his back hurt, but he didn't want to complain. If Linda were here he could imagine the two of them agreeing to go back down the hill and rent a cabin at the main campground, a decision that sounded much more appealing than continuing the hike. But maybe he was wrong. Maybe that kind of attitude was exactly what Linda had loathed about him—or rather, the old him.

He stopped and looked around at the seemingly endless stands of pine trees, their scent so stark he could taste it on the back of his tongue, and tried to force himself for a moment to just appreciate it all. He couldn't deny it was magnificent, but there was something unnerving about it, too, the weight of all that silence.

After another half-hour Terri stopped abruptly, unbuckled her pack, and swung it to the ground. "Screw this," she said. "This isn't really nature anyway. Let's cut to the chase. Someone will give us a lift."

There were not many cars, and the first few passed them without even slowing down. Robert had been sweating when they were walking uphill, but now that he was sitting in clammy clothes he found it was chilly despite the sunshine. At last an older woman in a pickup truck pulled over for them. Terri whooped with excitement, and they threw their packs in the bed of the truck and squeezed into the cab. As they drove up the hill, Robert realized he was relaxed for the first time all day. Having all those miles being eaten up by good old gasoline and tire rubber was an unexpected blessing. They soon reached the trailhead and retrieved their packs.

"Stay safe. Watch out for bears," the woman said.

"Okay, thanks!" Terri said. She wrestled her pack on and started down the path without hesitation. When Robert caught up with her, she smiled at him. "Only twelve miles left—easy-peasy," she said.

It became apparent very quickly that twelve miles would not be easy at all. The trail was narrow and winding and, at times, all but invisible. Winter had brought down a number of huge trees across the path that they had to scramble over or detour around, and in some places there was still a crust of icy snow on the ground that made walking treacherous. After an hour it was clear they would never make it to Grace Lake before sundown. Robert said as much to Terri, and she took the map out.

"Yeah, I guess you're right. But look, there's another campsite closer in. Logging Lake."

"I think the sign at the trailhead said it's closed."

"What does that even mean out here—no continental breakfast? We can just sleep there and go to Grace Lake in the morning. No one will know."

With an end in sight, they picked up their pace. Terri began singing at the top of her voice, which destroyed the peacefulness of the walk but which Robert found lifted his spirits. This would be fun after all.

When they reached the spot where the trail split toward the camp, however, there was a large sign blocking the path: "Wolf Area. A family of gray wolves has made its home at Logging Lake. To encourage this species to flourish, and for the safety of our hikers, Logging Lake Campground is closed until further notice."

"Well, shit," said Robert. "I guess we're going to Grace Lake after all."

"Hmm," said Terri. She walked around the sign, looking at it closely as though it required interpretation. "I mean, does that make sense? Wouldn't it make more sense to sleep here?"

"No," said Robert. "Because *wolves live here*."

"We can make a fire to keep them away. I'd much rather do that than be walking around wolf country in the middle of the night in the pitch-dark. We'll never see them coming."

"But it's their territory," Robert said.

Terri started walking toward the campground.

"Terri, come on."

"It'll be fine. We need to gather firewood before it gets dark."

Watching Terri light the fire was the high point of Robert's evening. She got a blaze going quickly, and for a moment he thought he had misjudged her. The firelight turned her hair bronze and threw golden flickers across her face that made her look like some kind of mysterious woodland spirit, and the sun set over the lake in a burst of pink and orange. But then the light started fading, and Terri was cursing as the pot of water she'd propped in the flames tipped over and spilled for the third time. Finally, they ended up eating lukewarm mush by the embers of the dying fire and crawling into the tent.

Robert had pictured this moment repeatedly in the days since Terri had proposed the trip. He had imagined he would be decisive and bold, drag the sleeping bags out of the tent, peel off those layers of hiking clothes in a way that would make her crazy with anticipation, make love in the chilly air under a sky full of stars. But now he had no interest in doing any of those things. It was more than chilly, it was downright cold, and his muscles were so stiff it felt like a tremendous effort even to remove his boots and strip down to his long underwear. *Say Yes to Everything,* he told himself, but what he wanted to say yes to was eight hours of sleep. In the profound darkness that settled over the tent Terri was all but invisible, but he could hear her soft, even breathing filling the space between them. What was she thinking? Was she waiting for him to do something? *Come on,* he told himself. *Get going.*

It was then that the wolves began to howl. They sounded uncomfortably close, perhaps only as far as the edge of the lake. Terri reached out in the darkness and grabbed his hand.

"What makes them sing like that?"

Hunger, Robert thought. *They're ready for a killing spree.* But he chided himself for being so pessimistic. No wonder Linda hated him; he couldn't enjoy anything. Terri wasn't worried about being eaten by wolves. Terri was *living in the moment.*

"Can I tell you something I've been wanting to tell you for a while now?" Terri said.

"Sure."

"The reason I might seem a little . . . shy sometimes . . . is because my last relationship was abusive."

Shy? Robert thought, but he said, "Oh, God. I'm so sorry. Your boyfriend hit you?"

"Everyone says that, like that's the only kind of abuse. He never laid a hand on me. I mean *spiritually* abusive. *Karmically*. Anyway, he wasn't my boyfriend."

Robert waited but she did not elaborate. "Wow," he said. This didn't seem like an adequate response, but it also felt inappropriate to tell someone who had just confessed to having been abused that they were full of shit. And who knew, maybe *he* was the one who was full of shit. Maybe he was spiritually abusive, too, and Linda was in bed with some guy right now telling him about all the years of spiritual abuse she had endured at Robert's hands. The thought made him feel sick, and he leaned in and kissed Terri. "I'm sorry that happened to you," he said.

"It has been the worst year up till now," she said. "The *worst*."

"Yeah," Robert said. The sound of the wolves was pushing him toward a state of profound anxiety, making it hard to think.

"I knew you would understand. You know what it's like to have someone destroy your life."

Robert leaned back from her. He knew he had never told Terri about Linda. He never discussed Linda with anyone anymore, even mutual friends of theirs. "What do you mean?"

"Don't worry. That's all over. This is the place where things start to get better." The wolves changed their pitch and Terri gripped his fingers even tighter, so tight it started to hurt. Robert pried his hand loose and put his arm around her.

"Don't be afraid," he said, though his voice sounded unconvincing even to him.

She laughed softly, more awe than amusement. "I'm not afraid. I think it's the most beautiful sound I've ever heard." She hummed a clear note, skimming up and down the scale until she landed in harmony with the wolves. Still holding his hand, she lay down, and Robert did the same. "Close your eyes. You can hear them even better."

Robert did as he was told. The weird music of Terri and the wolves filled the tent and knit itself into an endless, tuneless melody. He could not say how long it was before he fell asleep.

In the morning he woke early. Terri was not in the tent. Robert wriggled into his clothes and crawled outside.

A half-empty water bottle sat beside the remains of the fire. Robert continued down the trail to the outhouse, but once he finished taking a piss and rubbing his face with cold water from the lake it occurred to him that he should have passed Terri somewhere on the path. He went back to the campsite and called for her, but heard nothing. He decided to start getting ready for the day and returned to the tent, where he noticed that Terri's boots were still sitting by the door, her heavy wool socks balled up and stuffed inside.

For the first time he stopped and took stock of his surroundings. Both backpacks leaned against a rock beside the fire. He had a clear line of sight all the way down to the edge of Logging Lake and could not see any movement. He shouted Terri's name several times, but got no response.

A crawling, panicky tremble crept into his body. Where was Terri? She couldn't have gone far without boots. Unless she had other shoes, but this seemed unlikely. Or unless the wolves . . . but surely he would have heard something. Wouldn't he? He scanned the ground around the tent, looking for signs of a struggle. *Right, like you're some master tracker*. The ground was hard and gritty, and for all he knew you could drag an elephant across it with a backhoe and not leave any trace.

The thing to do was to be logical. Panicking was an Old Bob kind of thing to do. New Robert could handle this. Maybe she had just decided to go on a little morning walk and hadn't wanted to wake him. Maybe she liked to walk barefoot. Over sticks, in the snow. *Call her phone,* he thought, but when he fished his phone from his pack and tried to turn it on he found the battery had died during the night.

Surely he had to wait for her for at least a little while before he went for help. How ridiculous would he feel flagging down a ranger on the side of the road, only to come back and find Terri warming her toes by the fire? But three hours later there was still no sign of her. He had spent the time alternately calling for her, pacing the campground, and sitting in worried silence.

Now was the time to do something decisive. If he left now, he could reach the main road and hopefully flag down a car before dark. But why call in the rangers when he hadn't even tried to find Terri? That was a mistake, depending on someone else to take charge. For all he knew, she had gone a little ways down the path and twisted her ankle and was just hoping he found her. He had to take a look.

Reenergized, he grabbed a water bottle and set off down a trail that curved along the edge of the lake, intermittently calling for Terri and listening for a response. He could already imagine her weakened voice calling back to him, see himself lifting her from whatever patch of vegetation she had collapsed on and carrying her back to the campground. The trail was flat and easy, and he breathed deeply and nodded to himself. He could do this. He would find her.

But the lake was huge, and by the time he reached the far side, thick clouds were gathering on the horizon, cutting short the daylight he'd been counting on. In the sudden pall he picked up his pace, moving urgently back toward camp, his boldness draining away with the sunshine. Every chipmunk rustling through the bushes caused him a momentary panic as he froze in anticipation of a wolf springing onto the path. He was more frightened than he wanted to admit, and worst of all, he couldn't say what scared him most—the gathering darkness, Terri's disappearance, or being completely out of his depth. What if he got lost trying to get back to the campsite? What if he got struck by lightning? What was wrong with Terri to plan a trip like this to begin with?

Just as he reached the campground, it began to rain. First a few scattered drops, but almost immediately violent sheets of water. The tent was hunkered like a huge orange animal just beyond the fire ring, and he ran toward it, slipping in the newly formed mud. Once inside he zipped the doors shut and peeled off his wet clothes. His long underwear was still mostly dry, and he shoved the pile of sopping fleece into one corner and pulled both sleeping bags around him. As he did, he saw something fall to the floor of the tent: Terri's phone, gleaming a dull blue in the dim interior. He flipped it open, only to find that there was no signal. It was an ancient model, without games or photos or any of the other distractions he would have found on his own phone, but still, something about that small, concrete piece of civilization consoled him, and he cradled the phone against his chest, letting the light from the screen illuminate the cave of the tent.

Robert did not sleep that night, and with the first sunlight he headed out immediately. He abandoned the tent and all but a few supplies, ran practically the whole way back to the road, farther than he'd known he could run. The trucker who picked him up looked at him with concern but said nothing, just dropped him off at the road that led to the ranger station. As Robert walked the final mile toward the station, he found himself moving more and more slowly. The adrenaline of panic had worn off, and now he had to think about what came next. There would be alarm, suspicion, dozens of questions he was ill-prepared to answer. Just thinking about the impending drama made him nauseated, and he wished desperately for the comfort of something familiar here in all this wilderness.

He took Terri's phone from his pocket. One tiny little nub of a bar showed at the bottom of the reception scale. He dialed Linda's number and held his breath. She answered on the third ring.

"Lin," he said. "It's me. It's Bob."

The aftermath was both better and worse than he'd feared. The rangers went into action immediately, calling in a search team and notifying the police, and Bob told the same story again and again to various people. But after that initial flurry of activity, things slowed down. The search team— rangers, police, rescue volunteers, bloodhounds—found neither a living Terri nor a body. No one reported seeing her on the road back to the main entrance, or anywhere else in the park or surrounding towns. Two days later, a late-May snowstorm rolled through, which made searching difficult and drastically reduced any chance that Terri would be found alive. An expanded net of special investigators asked

Bob the same questions again, but his answers never changed and they seemed to believe him. The rangers hypothesized that Terri had gone off-trail, which meant she could have ended up almost anywhere. Her remains might turn up months or years later, discovered by some other unfortunate hiker who chose the same path.

When Bob arrived back at his apartment in Seattle—exhausted from a week of restless nights and police interrogation—Linda was outside waiting for him. He could only guess that she had learned his return date from one of the many articles that had been written in the Montana papers about Terri's disappearance and his role as a suspect. The same articles reported that the police had not been able to find anyone to provide information about Terri—no family or friends, no ex-boyfriend, no employer, only a few neighbors who said she had been quiet and withdrawn, timid to the point of vanishing.

Bob had not seen Linda in almost a year; she had grown her hair out and dyed it a rich auburn, and he would have walked right past without recognizing her if she hadn't jumped up from where she leaned against her car and grabbed his hand. She looked at him uncertainly for a moment before pulling him into a tight hug, saying, "My God, I can't imagine."

Bob knew he ought to tell Linda to go to hell; that it was too late and he didn't want anything to do with her; that calling her had been a moment of weakness. But the truth was he wanted nothing more than to walk to the door of what had been their apartment, to which she probably still had the damn *key*, for God's sake, and let her take care of everything.

They got married the following summer, a small ceremony with their parents and siblings and a handful of friends. "Of course, none of us were fooled by this whole 'we're calling it quits' thing that happened a couple of years ago," Linda's sister crowed during her toast, and while the rest of the guests laughed and Linda clasped Bob's hand, he looked down at his plate. *He* had certainly been fooled. He wasn't entirely sure he wasn't still being fooled, in some fashion he had just failed to identify.

In some ways, their renewed life together was everything he'd missed during the long months of Linda's absence: shared cooking and complaining about work and watching movies in bed at night. There were also some changes. They bought a cat, and new furniture; they spent more time out at plays and restaurants. But these shifts seemed to him superficial, and while Linda never complained anymore about being stagnated, Bob couldn't help but feel that her renewed attraction to him was based largely on Terri's disappearance. His connection to the bizarre tragedy gave him all the things she'd complained he lacked: an air of adventure, of mystery and possibility. He had occasional nightmares about Terri in which she emerged from Logging Lake, naked and muddy, her arms outstretched to embrace him, and others in which he came around a bend in the trail and found her crouched over a deer carcass, feeding from the ribs and grinning up at him with bloody teeth. When he woke from these dreams, breathing hard, every muscle in his body tense, Linda would inevitably give him a look of such tenderness that he wanted to scream.

If he and Terri had simply gone on their trip and come back home, Bob doubted he and Linda would ever have spoken again. The idea made him uncomfortable when he thought about it too much, which ensured that he never described to Linda that last night of the hiking trip, when he sat in the tent with Terri's phone in his hand, waiting for morning. Not long after the rain stopped, he had heard the wolves again, though farther away this time. Still, their calls pierced the thin walls of the tent, every wavering nuance audible, until the air seemed to thicken into tangible waves. Alone, shivering, clutching his knees against his chest, he heard what Terri had heard the night before—the sound was beautiful. Every hair on his body was lifted with the electricity of the wolves' voices, and he swore he could smell every item in the tent, from his wet socks to the tube of ChapStick in his pants pocket. And at the same time that he was saturated with the song's grandeur, he wanted it to stop.

He unzipped the front door of the tent and looked out. It was three in the morning, and he could see almost nothing. The dark glistening of the lake felt as ominous as the undulating edge of a black hole, and in that moment he felt

sure in his bones of one thing: Terri was dead, or at least she
was never coming back. The world outside the tent was exactly what she had come here looking for, a place that tran-
scended the lives they had both left behind in Seattle, and
it had somehow consumed her. He felt this was exactly what
Terri would have wanted, but it was not anything he could
bring himself to desire, even in its safer forms. If he were to
set foot outside, he would instantly be frightened, chilly,
bothered by the grit in his toes and the sticky film of sweat
on his skin. The thought struck him with a sharp bitterness
that quickly faded to acceptance. He didn't need a place
like this. He could be happy without it—happier, really. If
he died without ever seeing Paris he would not regret it for
a moment, something Old Bob had known instinctively.

A knock on the doorframe brought him out of the memory. Linda was standing there, looking at him, and he was
sitting on the edge of the bed with one sock in his hand and
the other still on his left foot.

"Oh, honey, what happened?" she said. "You look so
strange." And was there, or did he imagine it, some trace of
hope in her voice? Hope that he *did* have something strange
to offer her, something she would never truly seek out for
herself. The kind of hope that could be harbored only by
someone who had never been sung to sleep by wolves at the
edge of an unsoundable wilderness.

KILLER OF KINGS

for Leslie Brisman

The angel sits at John's bedside, a quill in her hand that may well be one of her own feathers. She raps the nib against the sheet and says, "John, John, John . . ." in that singsong, mocking way of hers, her perfect shoulders drooping: He's boring her. He sits up straighter against the pillows and tries to think, pressing his trembling fingertips to his temples, but inside his head is only a blank, hissing whiteness like a field of shifting snow.

"Imperfect?" she says. "Impious? Imperiled? Impressive?" Her voice has the low resonance of a cat's purr, so that he often feels it vibrating in his jaw.

"No," John says, "none of those," but what the right word is he just can't remember, it slips his grasp like so many things these days. The rate at which his body has betrayed him is shocking, and in moments like this he feels his age settle on him like a cloak of lead.

"John," she says, "we will be here all century at this rate. Tell me *something* or the Old So-and-So will be wroth with us both."

"Imprudent," he says, and she nods and moves the quill fluidly across the paper, but returns all too quickly to her posture of waiting, waiting, her anticipatory silence.

John knows he should be glad to see the angel; he has been blind for six years and should be glad to see anything, much less a messenger from Heaven. But she frightens him. Bitter white light seeps from her skin, and she has a faint scent about her like crushed granite and ice. There are times when he wishes he could close his eyes against her and return to the velvet darkness of his blindness.

The first time she appeared to him, John woke from a dream of dark and glassy seas and found the angel sitting in a straight-backed chair by his bedside. Without preamble she said, "I've come for your poem."

"Which one?"

"Oh, you know, the epic," she said, waving her fingers airily. "Fall of Man, Redemption, Forgiveness, et cetera. Your great work."

"I haven't written it."

"I'm well aware." A quill appeared in her hand, and a

board across her lap with a sheet of parchment and an inkpot. She smiled at him as she dipped the pen into the ink.
"Let's begin."

Now she looks at him with much less patience. "Something more, John," she says. "Epics are not made in a day,
and for all you know you will be dead tomorrow."

"I will not be dead tomorrow," says John. "Else you
would not be here with me." But his conviction does not go
further than his voice, and both of them know it.

It is centuries, now, since the angel began her work with
humans, and being close to them has invoked her curiosity,
if not her admiration. They are just so many stories patched
together, so many forgotten days encased in bone and meat.
One might unearth almost anything with enough searching.
Being a muse is mostly this—a sifting through of memories
to find something of merit, hauling it to the surface where it
can shine. The endeavor has, at the best of times, an exotic
appeal. Forgetting is a concept the angel knows only
through observation. Every moment of her long existence
echoes through her like the unfading peal of a bell, things
she would rather forget every bit as loud as those she would
remember.

When John was a young man he traveled across Europe,
and found himself one day visiting with Galileo. The great
scientist was blind, too, by then, and sick, only a few years
from death but still holding court in a borrowed villa in

Florence like some gnarled pagan king. If the doting nobles and scientists who surrounded him cared that he had been forced to recant his celestial cartography, that his home was little more than a comfortable prison, they gave no sign of it. Even John, wrapped in the arrogance of his youth, had been tempted to press his forehead to the floor at the astronomer's feet. But he had resisted, had fallen back on his Latin and his quips and tried to be witty, rather than reverent, until the old man interrupted him.

"A writer, are you?" Galileo said. "Cursed, even more than an astronomer. Full of strong opinions that will leave you cold in your old age."

"It may be so," said John, too shaken to think of any other reply.

"It is so. You're too young to know. Learn to smile in the daytime and write your heresies by candlelight, or you'll live to regret it."

Now John dreams he is back in Florence. He and Galileo stand face-to-face, two old men alone in a crowd of chattering admirers. John looks into the astronomer's dark eyes and the sounds of the room around them drop away. A misty dusk envelops them, until all John can see are the flames of the candles in the chandeliers high above, flaring brighter and brighter and then plunging like a meteor shower, raining down around the two of them to set the room afire.

The angel takes hold of John's hand and squeezes it until the bones ache. "Old man," she says, "stop daydreaming," and he startles awake and finds himself on the divan by the fireplace, the angel watching him as though she could see right through his skin.

Before he became blind, John would never have let someone else write his words down for him, not even an angel. The words were too important. Once upon a time, John fancied himself a killer of kings, and with them injustice, though he struck with sentences and not an executioner's ax. He could sit down at his desk at night and write until the sky turned gray with morning, mining truth and smelting arguments together until he had built a palace of reason. The talk in Parliament was all about whether the king should be tried as a traitor to the people, and everyone read John's pamphlets, whether they agreed with him or not. When the king was finally brought to trial and then to the chopping block, still holding his absurd little dog and mewling about his divine rights, John could not help but feel pride in having played a part in bringing it all about.

But these days, John is not so sure he is anything but a slayer of himself. Now *he* is the one who has been imprisoned. Tried for regicide, robbed of his books, barely saved from hanging by persuasive friends, and finally confined to this damp house, living under a new king despite his best efforts. His young wife and infant daughter dead within the year, he feels the world closing in around him, and wonders how long it can be before he follows them. The bones of John's feet throb with heat like red coals, and his own head might as well be severed for all the good it's doing him.

...

In the afternoons, Andrew, a younger colleague from John's glory days, sometimes comes to visit, and sits by John's bedside with a cup of tea rattling against the saucer in his hand. He brings with him all the gossip of Parliament. Andrew has done well for himself, has somehow escaped the censure that John fears will dog him to his grave, but John feels no jealousy, only gratitude that the two of them can still sit together like this and talk. He feels a waft of steam upon his face as he holds his own teacup to his lips; the fragrance of humid Darjeeling plantations rises to greet him.

"Will you write today?" Andrew says. "Shall I scribe for you?" But John shakes his head. He can think of nothing to say, though he knows his time is slipping through his hands like the tail of a rapidly shortening rope. It will burn his fingers with its passing and leave him clutching at empty air. The very thought makes him tired.

"Were we so wrong, Andrew, to want him gone?" he says.

"Hush, John," Andrew says, and John does not need sight to know the fear in his friend's face.

When John sleeps the angel walks long, winding paths through the city, though she could be anywhere she chose, some balmy island or sylvan waterfall. She feels the hardness of the ground beneath her feet, the dust that gathers on everything. She peers into windows and watches the inhabitants of the poorer quarters, their cold, cramped lives.

Some are happy, even in their squalor, but so many are sick
and weary. And everywhere she sees dirt, filth, such a quan-
tity of ugliness that she cannot find a reason for. She used to
know how to accept such things as wisdom, but she has
grown weary, too, that dirt has found its way into her somehow. Unspoken blasphemies poke against her insides like
shards of stone. She wants to say these things to John, sometimes, while he sits unspooling his stories. She has her own
stories to share, but that is not her task. Her task is only to
inspire, to help him create. Though she would not tell him
so, she is as much John's slave as she is the Lord's. In the
depths of night, she returns to his room, sits silently by his
bedside, watches the dreams scripting themselves against
the insides of his eyelids.

John is a boy in school and the master is reciting some dry
lesson of history, Pliny or Herodotus beaten to threads and
stretched into an endless droning. It is spring and the windows have been opened to air out the classroom; outside
the world is alive with the first traces of color and warmth.

In front of John sit two boys who hold the balance of the
class in their hands. One, named Hyslop, is the master's pet,
bland and eager and always ready with an answer, sitting
with his head cocked like a spaniel's. The other boy, Reede,
is a butcher's son, here by the charity of a wealthy patron,
fiercely proud and, John knows, ten times more intelligent
than Hyslop. He rarely speaks but there is a certain dark
gravity about him, and the other boys treat him with defer-

ence despite his poverty. He is facing the window, and has been for some time when the master asks a question. John has never been the best of students, though he loves books and reading, but even he knows the answer. He tentatively raises his hand as Hyslop leans forward in his seat, straining toward the front of the classroom, but the butcher's boy does not take his eyes from the window, as though he has not heard.

"Mr. Reede," says the master, "you seem to be otherwise engaged."

"It was Carthage, sir," the boy answers, but still he does not turn his head. John recognizes the audacity of this, but cannot help looking toward the window, searching for whatever holds Reede's attention, and he sees that many of his classmates are doing the same.

"And what is so interesting that you must leave off our discussion to gaze out the window like some lovesick girl?"

"The biggest hawk I ever seen, sir. In the oak tree. I want to see it fly again."

The master takes his stick from where it rests and cracks it against the table. All the other boys turn immediately to the front, flinching in their chairs, but John continues to watch Reede, who turns slowly, clearly reluctant to miss his chance at the hawk.

"Come here," says the master. Hyslop snickers, and in that moment John conceives a loathing for him that will last him the rest of his school days, perhaps the rest of his life.

Reede walks to the front of the room and, without being

told, holds out his hands, which the master paints with strokes until they bleed. Reede makes no sound but a rough grunt between clenched teeth, and when his punishment is concluded he returns to his seat, passing the window on his way, and only John catches his triumphant grin as the bird— indeed a magnificent one, dark brown with a mane of golden feathers—launches itself from the crown of the oak and plunges to the field below.

In days to come John will replay this moment, when his reading or his lessons lose his interest, or as he lies in bed at night waiting for sleep. Something about that grin delights and haunts him. Whereas before he might have respected Reede, he treats him now with a hushed reverence. A boy who cares more for the freedom to direct his own gaze than for the master's anger is a rare creature indeed.

The next morning John wakes early, while the house is still quiet. He reaches for the bedside table and his fingers find a pen, some parchment, his bell, and suddenly his mind flares into full wakefulness. He rings the bell for the maid, and as soon as he hears her footsteps in the doorway, he says, "I woke late last night and wrote. Read it back to me."

She takes the paper from his hand and the silence stretches out. "I can't," she says.

"My penmanship is not what it was, I'm sure, but try."

"It's not that, it's only . . . you've written all your sen- tences stacked on top of each other. I can't read a one of them, the paper's nearly black." Her voice is filled with sincere regret but something else, too. Call it doubt.

So that is it, then, the fruit of his night's inspiration, some hundred lines layered together like a surfeit of angels crammed onto a pinhead, crushing each other with their dancing.

Sometimes John thinks he has always known this poem, that it has underlain his life like the seeds of a field, waiting for the ray of sun that will call it forth into the world. Other days he thinks he will weave it together from images and sounds and bits of twine that he has found here and there through the years and stored in his pockets until he had need of them. There was even a time, decades ago now, when he began to write the poem, but it withered in his hands like a plucked flower. And so he learned to leave it alone, to let it grow in silence, until the silence consumed it, until the words fell asleep again beneath his skin. Now he wonders whether he will ever find them.

"Still nothing for me?" the angel asks. John looks especially tired today, but she can summon nothing more than irritation for his frailty. "What can I say, He will not be pleased."

"I need more time."

"You all say that. It is like one unending echo down here."

"I don't even know where to start."

"Start with yourself," she says. "That works for most of you."

The silence accumulates around them. Her patience is wearing thin. Sometimes she wishes he would simply die, and thereby secure her release.

"Have you always been a muse?" John says.

The angel sits up straighter. "I was a soldier," she says. "I fought in the Great War. Then I guarded the gates of Heaven. But eventually it was decided I should have some other occupation."

"It's only . . . You don't seem to like people. We must be very tiresome for you. Or perhaps it is just me."

"I pity people," she says. "Your lives are so filled with misery. Even for one such as you it is inescapable. Some-times this world appears to be *designed* for suffering. Sometimes—" She stops, draws a sharp breath. Her words shift within her like nervous birds. They long to go winging, and one loud noise will send the whole flock exploding out-ward, past the paltry gate of her tongue, into the world from whence they cannot be reclaimed. Her silence is all that stands between her and disobedience, and whatever pun-ishment that entails. John is looking at her now with a keen-ness she has not seen in him before. Instead of a broken old man, he looks like a dog who has scented prey.

"I asked for you especially," she says. "I heard a rumor about you. That you wrote a pamphlet saying rulers must be measured by their deeds, and prosecuted if they are found lacking."

"I did. I said that it was right to kill the king."

"Do you believe that still? That those who rule must give way if they are not just?"

Even she can hear the febrile edge that has crept into her voice, but John does not seem alarmed. For the first time, he looks at her as though he understands her. "I do still believe it," he says. "How glorious to be an angel, and know you serve the only truly just ruler to be found in all of creation."

The angel presses her lips together until they blanch, nods tersely, and looks away. "Hosanna," she says.

"John," says his mother.

She is somewhere behind him, in a hazy, firelight-soaked kitchen. His friends have gone off to play outside, but he has been sniffling lately and she has kept him home. The room smells of simmered beef bones and parsley. Farther back in the depths of the house John's father is playing the violoncello, a slow ribbon of notes that weave themselves into the brickwork, punctuated by periods of silence as he writes down the melody. John breathes on the windowpane and swipes at it with the cuff of his shirt to clear the frost away. "John," his mother says again, but he barely hears her.

Outside, crouched on the windowsill, is the cooper's cat, a big marmalade brute named Sully, now spotted white with snowflakes. Between his forepaws he holds a bird. It is a plain brown sparrow with rumpled feathers and eyes blinking rapidly. Sully moves his paws apart and the bird sits stunned for several seconds before it leaps for the sky. John swears he can feel those wings tickling against the inside of his chest; his heart leaps with the bird, but before it has risen a handsbreadth, Sully swipes it down again, pins it into the snow. The windowpane slowly frosts over and John does not wipe it clean again.

But John can't remember this now. It's too long ago, he's too old; that snow-dappled cat has faded from his memory, as has the bird and its struggles. Only a pair of ragged wings remain, fluttering in the darkness of his mind, harrying him onward to something he cannot yet name.

The next time John sees the angel, he says, "I had a thought."

"Yes?" she says.

"I thought that I would start the story in Hell, not Heaven. With the Fallen."

Her face remains impassive as a rock.

"With the Devil," he says, lowering his voice and raising his eyebrows, vamping for her attention. She smirks before she regains her composure.

"That is your choice," she says.

"He must have been furious."

"I have heard."

"What else have you heard?"

She looks steadily into his eyes and picks her words carefully. "Rags and scraps. There is no gospel in Hell."

"I would like to hear it anyway," he says.

She nods slowly, her whole face relaxing as if she has

been holding her breath until this moment. "That is your choice," she says again. "If you ask me to tell you, then I must." She seems as though she is speaking to someone else, her voice high and clear, but then it drops back to its regular low rumble and she begins to tell him stories.

By day's end they have filled a score of pages, and the angel reads them aloud, her rough voice thrumming with their cadence. When she reaches the last word they look at each other with excitement and dread, to see the apocryphal tale so sharply alive on the paper, crackling with pain and fire and recrimination. In that moment John realizes that for all her world-weariness, her millennia of existence, she is younger than him in one way: She has never known firsthand the consequences of rebellion. He feels suddenly protective of her. *Look at me,* he thinks. *See what happens to dissidents. Listen to the story you are telling.* But before he can speak the angel looks up and says a quick, soft word he cannot understand, and then the white light of her presence is snuffed. John sits alone in the darkness, listening to the muted crackle of the logs in the grate, the soughing of the wind outside the house.

That night he sleeps fitfully, falls back to the dark ocean of his old dreams, but the waves that hold him now are rough ones, pitching and heaving as though a great storm approaches. When at last he wakes, he feels as if he has washed up on some distant shore. He opens his eyes, looks to his bedside, and is startled to see a new face looking back at him. This angel sits just as the other did, with parchment and a quill poised upon his lap, but his face is blandly pleasant, and the radiance he emits is more like sunshine than lightning.

"Hello," he says, "shall we begin?"

"Where is she?" John says.

The angel raises his eyebrows in mild surprise, as though the question were a strange one, even rude. "Called away. Are you ready?"

John is shaken. He wants to call her back but realizes he does not even know her name. "We were working. I want . . . . We were writing."

"Let us move along from there," the angel says smoothly. There is something inexorable about his soft insistence. "Perhaps, later, you will wish to change that part. Let us write about the glories of Heaven," he says, and John, stuttering, agrees.

Years pass before the book is finished. When at last it is complete, John asks Andrew to read it back to him. As John listens to the first pages, it is like hearing someone else's voice—the voice of his own beloved, seditious angel, though he has not seen her again in all these many years. He is moved by the pain and beauty of the lines, but pricked, too, by their blasphemous edge: angels stalking about the Garden like bullies; the Father and Son a pair of sparkling tyrants; and the Devil filled with despair to wring the heart, clothed in beautiful metaphors and adamantine defiance.

John hears in the mosaic of the poem all the images he has collected throughout his life, but something else as well— another tone, another thread that speaks in sympathy with his own heart but in a bolder voice. It frightens him; he knows as well as anyone the price of antagonizing kings. He waves Andrew to silence, says to him, "I must make it clear that these are her words."

"Whose words? Clear to whom?"

John shakes his head. He finds himself near tears. "We will fix it. We will give her the credit due to her. It wants an explanatory prologue, or an invocation of the muse. It wants her name upon it." Even as he says it John asks her forgiveness, for being unwilling to own his complicity in what they have created, to accept his share of the punishment. *You ask too much of a sick old man,* he thinks, *you who will never be sick or old.*

Andrew turns a few pages of the manuscript and the parchment whispers and scrapes against itself. "Whatever you believe is best, John. I cannot think how it could be improved, but who knows a work like its creator?"

"It must be clear," John says again, and taking the bell from his bedside table he rings it violently to call the maid, filling the room with its peals.

"Peace, John, she is coming," Andrew says, and lays a hand upon his arm. In the quiet that follows John hears the footsteps in the hallway, rapidly approaching, the rustle of her skirts as she brings the inkpot and the quill.

ALL THE NAMES FOR GOD

Abike stands in the doorway of my room and says, "I want to see my parents. Will you come with me?"

I don't answer at first. I meet her gaze in the mirror but keep wrapping my skirt. Abike's parents have moved to Abuja. My family is also in Abuja now. She knows this. Though I have called them and written letters, I haven't seen my family since Abike and I were captured, eight years ago, when we were just sixteen. She knows this also. It is not a small favor to ask. I finish dressing.

"All right," I say.

We hitchhike for two days, take a bus once we reach Karu. On Friday, at dusk, when the National Mosque is just lighting up against the sky, we arrive in the city. I haven't been to

Abuja since I was a child, maybe nine or ten years old, when I came here on a weekend trip with my parents. I peer from the window of the bus at the towering buildings, the sheer volume of people.

"Let's have a night out," I say. "We'll do our visiting tomorrow."

"Sure," says Abike. Her relief tells in her shoulders. "Where do we start?"

We start at the Hilton. We are still in our country clothes, the same worn clothes we garden and market and fetch water in, and small ridges of dried mud fall from our shoes onto the polished floor of the lobby as we enter.

"Do you want to do it, or should I?" Abike says.

"As you like."

She nods and heads to the reception desk. The man working the counter is wearing a black suit and a crisp white shirt and has the haughtiness so common among people who serve the rich for a living, as if they are superior just from being near other people's money. From across the room he has been scowling at us, with our dirty, rumpled clothes, but when Abike approaches and leans toward him, he becomes nervous.

"We'd like to check in," she says in English. "The name is Okonkwo."

He searches the computer for a moment. "I'm sorry, madam. I don't see anything under that name for tonight."

Abike frowns. "What kind of service is this? We've had reservations for months."

The man taps at the keyboard weakly. "No, I'm very sorry."

"Well, don't you have anything? Is the hotel full?"

"We have some rooms on the ninth floor with two queen beds."

"That's fine. But we're very upset. You should let us have it for free."

A family of white tourists has stepped into line behind us, a fat mother and father and two skinny teenage girls wearing torn jeans and pouts. The receptionist shifts uncomfortably from foot to foot and looks away, but Abike snaps her fingers and he turns back to her. One of the teenagers giggles, but the man shows no sign that he's heard her. He is eyeing Abike as though she is a dog and he is a cornered rat.

I've seen this face many times before, on many men. This man is used to difficult people, rich people, demanding foreigners. He is used to coolly and politely declining unreasonable requests, but this time he finds he can't do it. He looks as though he would like to cry. Abike taps her finger slowly against the stone counter and for a moment even I believe I can hear the click of manicured nails, though I'm looking at the blunt tips of her fingers. She's very good.

"I can't," he pleads. "I'm not allowed to give rooms for free."

"Really?" Abike's displeasure rolls out in waves. She sets one fingertip lightly on the cuff of his suit and he flinches.

Another employee comes to ask him a question, but he doesn't seem to hear her.

"We would really like that room," Abike says, and lets the silence accumulate between the two of them like a growing weight.

"Well, it's our mistake," the man says at last. He puts two key cards in a paper sleeve and hands them to Abike.

"Thank you," she says. She smiles at him and he smiles back idiotically. His relief is overwhelming him; he's so grateful that he has been able to give her what she wants. He nods his head eagerly and she turns to me and picks up her duffel. The tourist family stares at us as if we are museum exhibits, and Abike's eyes are laughing as we head to the elevator.

Abike and I weren't close before we were kidnapped, but we come from the same village. She was the kind of girl who could be your best friend one minute and ridicule you without mercy the next. She thought she was special because she had cousins in Chicago who sent her tattered American magazines with articles about sex, and because during our lunch break at school she always put on more makeup than anyone's mother would allow and rolled up her uniform skirt until her thighs showed. So, of course, all the boys looked at her like she was a goddess when we sat outside, and somehow the teachers never caught her at it. Away from school she was always prim and proper. If she passed my family in the street, she would say in her prissy English, "Hello, Mrs. Layeni, Mr. Layeni. I hope you are well," and when she had gone my mother would say, "See? What a fine girl she is. So polite."

We were at church when the soldiers came, a group of us helping the Sunday school teacher get ready for her class. Abike was setting the Bibles on the desks. My phone chimed, and I saw it was a text from my mother, who knew I was in Sunday school, who knew I was not even supposed to be looking at my phone. The message said, "Come home now now." As I was staring at it, the phone began to ring, and then the door crashed open.

At first we thought the men were government soldiers, that it was some kind of emergency and we were going to be evacuated. Then one of them walked up to Mrs. Adeyemi and shot her in the face. We all screamed and tried to run, but there was another man blocking the door. The soldier who had shot our teacher looked at her body on the floor and kicked it.

"That's what you get for poisoning these girls' minds," he said.

I thought, *Why is he talking to her when she's already dead?* I had thoughts like that the whole day, very rational thoughts, like my brain was trying to throw weight on the other side of a scale against all the madness that was happening around me.

The men told us to go outside. We found trucks waiting,

filled with girls our age and with more soldiers. The men took our phones and any money we had. They pointed with their guns and said, "Get in."

We rode for hours while the daylight faded into dusk, onto smaller and smaller roads, until we were moving through the forest. You could hear night birds and monkeys all around, calling to each other.

My friend Naomi was next to me and she said, "We should jump out now, Promise. They might not even notice. We could hide in the leaves and they'd never find us in the dark." I nodded, but neither of us jumped. I had never been anywhere this remote, and the wildness of the place terrified me. If I had known what the next few years would be like, I would have jumped even if I could see a lion waiting in the shadows, but back then I was still hoping we would get to go home. Abike was in the same truck with us, crying and sniffling until finally one of the men said, "Shut up back there," and she was quiet. Later she told me she thought we would all be killed, that they would douse us in gasoline and set us on fire. I don't know where she got that idea. We had never heard of any such thing happening to anyone. But in a way she was not wrong; parts of us would be burned away forever.

Our room at the Hilton overlooks the pool, its cool blue water undulating against the stifling blackness of the surrounding night. We take showers and ransack the minibar. Abike pulls a red dress and a pair of high heels from her duffel and starts steaming the dress with the iron. My dress is black and stretched too tight to wrinkle. We share a lipstick and look at ourselves in the mirror.

"My mother would shit herself," says Abike at last.

"Let's go," I say.

We walk down the street until we find a disco, packed with tourists and the girls who flock to tourists. We dance for an hour and then go to the bar to cool down. There are two girls chatting up some white men, Americans or maybe Brits. The girls have their long hair blown straight and look like they've been injecting themselves with some chemical to make their skin lighter. They pass a cigarette back and forth between them.

I stand too close to the nearest man. He looks up, surprised, but when I tap the bar with my finger he smiles at me and asks if I'd like a drink. I tell him I would. The party girls scowl. They can't understand how these men can even be looking at us, with our dark skin and our close-cropped hair. I smile at them; it's a look women anywhere recognize from other women, a dangerous shark look. They shrink back against each other and sullenly sip their drinks. Abike gulps a shot of vodka and orders another. I turn to the man beside me.

"Give me some money," I say.

"What?"

"Money," I say louder.

"You want another drink?"

"No." I hold his gaze and breathe deeply. The noise of the club disappears. The angry stares of the party girls dissolve at the edge of my vision. All I can see is this man, and all he can see is me. "Not for a drink. Not for anything. Just give it to me."

He doesn't reply, but he fumbles in his pocket, takes some bills, and presses them into my hand. I slip them into my purse without looking, and blink. The music roars back to life. The party girls are gone, and Abike is sliding from her barstool, saying something I can't hear and pulling me toward the ladies' room.

The next morning, we get dressed to see our mothers. Abike has a green-and-yellow dress. The smell of our house is still lingering in the folds of the cotton; she pulls it over her head and begins to wind her *gele* around her temples while I put on my own dress, red and blue. We pleat our *geles* and pin them so we are crowned just so. Again we look at each other in the mirror. Abike nods. Already I'm beginning to feel uncomfortable. When we look like this it's too easy to see those girls we were—young, happy, helpless. These are the clothes our mothers would have dressed us in for holidays if we had finished growing up with them. We would have found them old-fashioned and complained that we wanted Western dresses. But now that we can dress as we please, we are more determined than ever to meet our parents in costumes they will find acceptable, to look something like the women they would have wanted us to grow into.

We go to Abike's parents' apartment first. Unlike me, she has visited before, so she has some idea what to expect. We stand in the lobby of their building and she stares at the elevator doors with an expression I can't read. At last I reach out and push the button to go up. "There are worse things," I tell her, and she laughs and steps into the elevator. When she is gone, I go outside and get in a taxi to find my own family's place.

The first day after we were kidnapped, we stayed in the forest, and the men made us pray all day long. They did not give us food, and only enough water to keep our tongues moving. Their camp had a tall post that showed which direction Mecca was in, and we had to kneel facing it while a man named Bashir shouted out all the names they used for God, and commanded us to repeat them: *the Compassionate, the Merciful, the Controller, the Strong, the Abaser, the Avenger, the Forgiver* . . . Ninety-nine words that were foreign and clumsy in our mouths. While we prayed, Bashir paced back and forth. If he thought someone was not saying the words correctly or not paying attention, he hit her with a stick or shouted in her face until she cried. We were so afraid of him then, as if being shouted at was something to fear.

Then we began to learn the long list of things that were

haram, forbidden. Praying to Jesus: haram. Uncovering your head: haram. Laughing: haram. Whispering to the other girls: haram. Looking a man directly in the eyes: haram. Unless he told you to, and then: *halal,* permitted. Unless he didn't like the way you looked at him, and then, of course, you had to be punished.

They had a lot of punishments. If they were feeling lazy they would just slap you, or threaten to kill you. They would threaten to kill you for anything—too much spice in the food you had cooked, not keeping the camp clean enough, not smiling enough or smiling too much. But that was just when they couldn't be bothered to try harder. There was one girl who offered herself to one of the soldiers, thinking he would protect her. So he enjoyed her, but then he pulled her out into the middle of the camp, still naked, and shouted for the other men to come and witness what a brazen whore she was. They took turns beating her until you could not even recognize her face. She died three days later. And things like this happened all the time: to girls who tried to run, girls who were "defiant" or "shameless." After a while, you put your effort into learning not to see them while you looked right at them, into singing songs in your head so you didn't hear them scream.

Still, we thought someone would come for us. There were stories—girls ransomed by their parents, negotiated for by the government. Even if we wouldn't admit it to one another, we still had hope that there was a way out. And then, one night, we woke to hear the men shouting. There were torches moving in the darkness, the sound of gunfire. The next thing I knew, I was being pulled to my feet, dragged out of the tent where we slept. Abike was beside me, and I saw her grabbed by another man, his arm around her throat, a gun in his free hand. The men looked crazed; they were yelling and cursing at us to move faster, and all around girls were crying and asking what was going on. The men half pushed, half dragged us to the edge of camp, and there I saw what I had been wanting to see for the past four months: a line of soldiers in government uniforms, their guns pointed at the camp, shouting at the men who held us to drop their weapons. Except the men did not listen, and you could see that the government soldiers were panicked. The man holding me began to fire at the soldiers, his arm like a bar across my throat, holding me in front of him, and I struggled but could not get loose. In front of me the soldiers were dying, their chests and heads bursting, and soon any that were left turned and retreated, and the men in the camp shouted after them, triumphant. At last, the man holding me let me go.

It had probably been only five minutes since I was asleep, but I felt as if the shooting had been going on all night. I was half-deaf from the gunfire and I fell to the ground crying, trying to get my breath back, but the man who had held me pushed me with the toe of his boot and said, "Start moving those bodies. There. Pile them together." So I did. Because I knew they would not hesitate to kill anyone who displeased them that night. Abike and I worked together, grabbing legs, arms, dragging the bodies to the pile. One of them wasn't even dead, though he was bleeding plenty. He watched us and said nothing, his eyes moving slowly in his face. Probably he was hoping the same thing we had always hoped: that if he just stayed quiet, they would overlook him, and he would find a way out. But it was dawn, and all around us the forest was getting lighter. We knew in the morning the men would set the bodies on fire.

At last, they let us rest. I sat on the ground, my head against my knees, and Abike sat a little distance off. We couldn't even look at each other. My hands and arms were sticky with blood, my clothes soaked with it. The flies would not leave me be, but I was too tired to chase them away. Someone sat next to me and I lifted my head long enough to see that it was one of the men, the one named Karim. I knew I shouldn't disrespect him by ignoring him, but in that moment I didn't care; even if I died for it, all I wanted was to be left alone. I could hear him breathing, under the buzz of the flies. Then he put his hand on the back of my head. "Promise," he said.

They didn't often call us by our names. I hadn't even realized he knew my name. He patted my head in a way I imagine was supposed to be comforting, but it made me feel unclean to have him touching me at all. I flicked my eyes up past the tops of my knees and I could see Abike, watching us but not directly, her whole body tense.

"Did you not have any Muslim friends in your village?" he said to me.

I nodded, barely moving my head. It seemed like a trick question. They never asked us about our villages. In fact, my best friend had been a Muslim girl named Fatima. She was as shy as a dormouse, but we always understood each other. Sometimes on Saturdays we would ride in the back of my uncle's truck to the nearest town and walk through the market together holding hands, and half a day would pass where we would not say anything and be perfectly content.

Karim moved closer, and looked at me earnestly. "Then you know what life you could have," he said. "You're upset, but if we hadn't killed those soldiers, do you know what they would have done? They would have killed all of us, and taken you back to your village."

Yes, I thought. In that moment, I could imagine my village more clearly than I had in months: the smell of the incense in church, the passing breeze of the fan as I sat behind my desk at school, the taste of Abike's lipstick when she let me borrow it, of *akara* straight from my mother's frying pan. *Yes, they would have done that.*

"And then you would never have come to understand how great Allah is, and your soul would be lost. So these men had to die. Allah wouldn't allow it to be any other way. Don't cry."

I nodded my head again at this, but I hid my face in my knees and cried harder. Thinking about home, even for those few seconds, had torn apart some shell I had gathered around me over the months since our capture. Usually I didn't let myself imagine it. It was only some place I had known in another life, and might see again if I lived long enough.

A moment later Karim shoved me forward, so that I went sprawling onto my face. "You're a stupid girl," he said. "All of you, stupid girls. Your crying only shows how ungrateful you are."

After that, we stopped waiting for anyone to come for us.

Several weeks after the government soldiers attacked, the men decided that our camp was too vulnerable; they split us up and took us to different towns. Before we left, most of us were married off, myself to Karim, Abike to Bashir, standing in the middle of camp while a man with a long white beard recited the same ceremony again and again.

Do I even need to say that we were raped? The only question was whether you were raped before or after being married. The men thought they had been saints for waiting a few months to "reeducate" us before posing this question; this proved to them that they were not just bandits but true followers of Allah. If you refused to convert and be married—you could refuse—then you were an infidel whore and they could do as they liked with you. If you were married, then of course you could not refuse your husband, or couldn't expect him to care if you did. It was a choice of being raped by one man or many, not a very difficult choice.

I never saw most of the girls again, but Abike and I went to the same small village in Borno State. Our husbands were boyhood friends, our houses next door to each other. We frequently ate together, the four of us, Abike and I sitting silently while Bashir and Karim laughed and joked with each other.

One day, Abike called me to her house to eat lunch with her. Our husbands liked this, when we did normal wifely things, inviting friends over for lunch. It made them feel like maybe we were normal wives, like we had chosen them, rather than being forced to marry them. They were eager to believe this. For their own sakes, they should have been more eager to see the truth: that we despised them.

Bashir came into the room. "Husband," Abike said, "please sit down with us." He sat down and she smiled at him and looked into his eyes. She began tapping her hand on the table, gradually slowing her pace. At first I thought she was going to say something, but she didn't, just kept staring at Bashir. Her hand was resting on the handle of the teakettle but she didn't pour any tea. Her husband shifted in his seat, as though he had sat down on something that prickled, but then he was still again. After a long time, Abike said, "You should lie down on the bed and say the names of God a hundred times. Say them very slowly, and don't miss any. Promise and I are going to sit outside."

Bashir blinked and nodded. He got up and walked to the bed and lay down facing the wall, and we heard him start to say the names of Allah. I just stared at him for a long time. I was so shocked I could barely breathe. I didn't know any word for what she had done to him, but I could see that she had done it. "Come," she said, and she led me to the door and out into the sunshine.

The young man who opens the door to my parents' apartment raises his eyebrows at me and moves more solidly into the doorframe, as though he expects me to push past him. For a moment, I think I've got the wrong address. In the past four years, in the many letters and phone calls I've exchanged with her, my mother has asked me dozens of times to come home. I've made any number of excuses about why I couldn't, and now I wonder if, when I've finally worked up the courage, they've moved somewhere else and neglected to tell me.

But over the man's shoulder, I can see a table and on it a blue-and-pink bowl of fruit, the same bowl my mother has had my entire life. I look at the man again and realize this is my brother, George. The last time I saw him he was eleven years old, scrawny and missing a tooth. Now he is nineteen, heavily muscled in his arms and chest, wearing a Che Guevara T-shirt and knockoff designer jeans. He leans against the doorjamb and says, "You looking for my parents? They're not home."

My hand flutters against my chest. "Promise. It's Promise," I say, though my throat is so tight I can barely speak.

Still, he stares at me for a second before he says, "Oh.

Oh, you?" He hugs me tightly, lets go again and takes my hand. "Come inside."

He walks into the room and there's a carelessness in the way he moves, a looseness in the joints. I realize he's drunk. He sits on the sofa and looks up at me without a trace of nerves, gestures vaguely at the other chairs in the room. I sit in one and he takes an orange from the bowl on the table and begins to peel it.

"So, you decided to come and see us."

"I felt like it was time." He nods as though this makes perfect sense, though it doesn't, even to me. "Where are Mom and Dad?"

"I don't know, I was sleeping when they left. Probably just at the store or something. Want a drink?"

"Sure."

He goes to the kitchen and comes back with two glasses, then to his bedroom for a bottle of Scotch. We clink glasses and throw the liquor back. I try to remember what I know about this grown-up George, what my mother has told me. He was supposed to be at the university this fall but couldn't be for some reason. He's been working somewhere instead—a restaurant? A copy shop? A week ago I could have told you, but right now my mind is blank. I don't know what to make of this man, how to connect him to anything I know about my brother. Whatever I expected coming home to be like, it was not this, my brother watching me with nonchalant amusement while we get drunk in the middle of the day.

Behind me there is muted conversation from the hallway, the click of the lock as the door opens. Before I can
turn around, I hear my mother's voice, sharp, saying,
"George, I have told you for the last time, keep your dirty
girls out of my house." She walks quickly toward me and as
I turn to face her, she is shoving a bag of groceries into my
father's arms. Whether she was planning to strike this "dirty
girl" or just shove her into the hallway I never find out, because when she sees my face, she says, *"Chei!"* and claps
her hand over her mouth. Her eyes fill with tears and instead of trying to embrace me, she staggers back a step, for
which, I find, I am grateful. I don't know how to put my
arms around her; I need that little distance. I try to smile at
her but I can't, I only want to weep. I say, "Hello, Mama,
hello, Dad," and my father hugs me hard against his side
with the groceries still cradled in one arm.

Without Abike's help, I would never have been able to go
home. She taught me what she knew, that way of controlling
a man that I had no name for.

"How did you learn it?" I said.

"Do you know Onyeka, that woman who lives at the edge
of the village?"

I nodded. Onyeka was a prostitute. Not that anyone said
it, but she walked through town with her head uncovered,
wearing makeup, laughing too loud. She touched all the

men in ways we wouldn't dare. I often saw her in the market, but of course we were not supposed to talk to her.

"She can do it," Abike said. "She taught me. I thought she was just boasting. But it works. How else could she go around like she does in a place like this?"

"But why were you talking to her anyway?" I said.

Abike looked away. She nodded her head silently, as though replying to some other question I couldn't hear. Finally, she said, "I went to ask her how to get rid of a baby. Anyway, I'll teach you. How to do both."

So she tried to explain it to me. She said to start with simple things: make a man scratch his nose, or look away. Things he won't question, things he might do anyway. But for months I felt nothing, like I was just staring at Karim, and worried all the time that he would ask me what the hell I thought I was looking at.

"It's like anything else," Abike said. "You have to practice."

So I kept trying. And after a while, I began to understand. It felt like reaching out with your hands in a dark room, feeling for something you knew was there but could not see, except the room you were reaching into was another person. After a year, if I concentrated, I could sometimes persuade Karim that he wanted to go out instead of staying home, that he was too tired to touch me when he lay down next to me at night. If I said I wanted to visit with Abike, he didn't object anymore, even if it was time for me to cook his supper or wash the clothes.

Abike and I started to spend more time together, to take longer and longer walks around the village, but we got too bold. One day, we were sitting in the kitchen drinking our tea when the door slammed open and my husband walked in. Abike grasped my leg beneath the table, but her face remained calm. She smiled at him and welcomed him and asked if he would have some tea with us. He pushed past her into the back room where Bashir was lying in bed and said, "Bashir, get up." Bashir didn't move, just kept talking quietly to himself. Abike and I stood behind Karim, huddled together.

"He's praying, you shouldn't disturb him. He tells me never to bother him when he is praying," Abike said, but Karim shook Bashir roughly by the shoulder.

"Get up!" he said. Then he turned and struck Abike hard across the face so that she fell to the floor. "You damned witch," he said in English, and I thought, *Yes, that is the word. That is what we are.* He took me by the arm and shook me. "You, too? You think you'll turn me mindless like you've done with him? This man is like a brother to me, and what have you bitches done to him?" He shook me harder. I screamed and wept but all the time I was thinking, *Just look at me. Just look at my eyes for one moment and I'll end this all.* Abike didn't make any sound and I was afraid for her; I wondered if he had killed her. He grabbed me by the chin and said, "Stop crying and answer me."

I looked at him, reached out into his eyes, deep, deep into him until I could feel the center of him, and what I found there I squeezed and crushed. I was too frightened to be subtle. He let go of me, but I leaned toward him, I kept his eyes. "Go sit on the bed with Bashir," I said, and he staggered backward until he found the mattress. "Help him say the names of God." I went back to Abike. She was sitting up now. She looked up at me and smiled and her front tooth was cracked.

"We have to go," I said.

"We're taking them with us," she said. "You know what kind of evil they'll get up to if we leave them alone." She gathered all the money from my house and hers, and we took our husbands by the hands and walked out of the village.

We went to a new town, a place where no one knew us and big enough that no one had time to care who we were. We got a house where we could live together, mobile phones, new clothes. I could have called my parents right then. I hadn't spoken to them in three years and I knew they must wonder what had happened to me, even wonder if I was still alive.

And I know what you're thinking, what anyone would think: Why didn't you run straight home? The truth was that we couldn't bear to see anyone we knew, knowing the things we had done. We had killed babies and soldiers, had watched as girls wrapped themselves with bombs to go to the market where they would murder people like our mothers and fathers, and we did nothing to stop them. We had spat and screamed at the other girls in camp when they looked for comfort, had blasphemed, lied, spoken against everything we once believed in. We might have sold our own siblings to gain our freedom if someone had given us the chance. We had nights where we did not fight back the little bit we could have, where we did not even say, "Please, no," and where we imagined a new life that went something like this: Go along, praise Allah, have clean clothes and enough to eat, raise some militant's baby like any other woman raising a baby, forget about how it all started. When these things have never happened to you, you think, *I would rather die*. But the truth is that it is not so easy to decide to die. And when, suddenly, you have the option to live again, that is not so easy either.

When my parents are finished crying, my mother cooks supper for me, all the recipes I haven't tasted since I was sixteen. I stand in the kitchen with her and chop vegetables while my father and George watch football in the next room. I know she doesn't need my help, but I don't know what to say to her and it feels good to have something to occupy my hands. As we work, she talks about George, raising her voice now and then when she wants to make sure he hears her.

"He's too busy for school," she says. "Busy drinking and chasing girls. You remember, he was such a good boy, and what happened? He's wasting his life."

"It's mine to waste," he says from the living room, and from the grim tone of his voice I can tell this is a fight they've already had many times, one where the heat of the argument has given way to simmering resentment. My father tells him to be quiet and my mother hands me an onion for the chopping board.

She makes enough food for a dozen people, and when she has it all on the table, my father claps his hands and breathes deeply before he says grace. He always did this, but I'd forgotten about it until just now. George and I would roll our eyes at each other just before we folded our hands to pray. I look at my brother and he meets my eye and, for a moment, he smiles, the same mischievous smile he had at eleven, and I can see him just as he was, as though no time has passed. My father thanks God for bringing me back to their house, and my mother squeezes my hand in hers as though she could knit our flesh together.

After we eat, my mother says, "I'll get some sheets. You can sleep on the sofa."

"I have a hotel room."

"No," she says. "You have to sleep here. What kind of mother lets her daughter sleep alone at a hotel?"

The cushions of the sofa are too soft, the night too full of city sounds. I lie awake, still dressed, listening to my parents' breathing in the next room for perhaps an hour before a wedge of yellow light spills into the hall from George's bedroom. He steps softly into the living room and stands looking down at me.

"You awake?"

"Yes."

"Want to get out of here? Have some fun?"

"Sure."

"All right, come on." He holds out his hand to help me up from the couch and I'm surprised all over again by the strength and size of him. When I'm standing, he looks me up and down and says, "Do you have something else to wear? Something less . . . you know?"

"Yes."

"Good," he says. "I don't want people to think I brought my aunt to a party."

"Shut up," I tell him, but I'm smiling in the darkness.

From outside I text Abike: *Need a break? Going to a party, meet me there.* I ask George for the address and send it to her, then we hail a cab and head out across the city.

The party is in a basement apartment in the far western suburbs. A few lamps with pink shades cast a dim light over the main room, where people are packed tight together and dancing. George disappears into the kitchen to get us drinks. I look around for Abike but don't see her. The people here are anywhere from eighteen to thirty, college students and office workers and new arrivals who've come to give the big city a try. They all look impossibly young to me. George presses a bottle of beer into my hand and says something I can't hear. Soon he is dancing with a girl in a low-cut dress, leaving me to my own devices. I retreat to the

kitchen, where a man smiles at me and asks me where I'm
from.

"Near Matazu," I reply, though the village where George
and I grew up feels like it's several lifetimes away. I tell myself, *It's not that hard. It's just talking. Just talk to him.* But
it's been a long time since I talked to a man for fun. I take a
deep gulp of my beer and let the alcohol relax me, and soon
we are chatting, like normal people. Others join us and an
hour goes by before I go to look for George, and finally spot
him on the far side of the living room, standing in a corner
with Abike.

George is smiling but he looks dazed. He is staring down
at Abike and opening his wallet. She stands with her hand
out, smiling in a self-satisfied way, as George counts a pile of
pink and blue bills into her palm. He stops and she taps the
money with her finger, *more,* and he starts again. For a moment I stand where I am, unable to move, just watching
them. Then I am across the room in three strides, shoulder-
ing my way through a throng of dancers and grabbing the
money from her hand. "No," I say.

Abike laughs. "*Peche,* relax, don't we always share?"

I shove the money back into George's wallet and close
his fingers around it. Abike looks at me like I have lost my
mind, like she would be angry if she weren't so surprised.
"No, no, it's George," I tell her. "It's my brother." What I
want to say is, *He's different. He's not here to beat us or rape
us or even lie to us. He's a good boy.* But he's not a boy any-

more, and I can feel tears hot in my eyes and my fingers curling into fists, as though there were someone to strike.

Abike looks at the floor. "Sorry," she says, and turns and walks away before either of us can say anything else.

George stands there blinking, clutching his wallet. "I think I've had too much to drink," he says. "Who knew it was possible?" He smiles his little-boy smile at me. "Is your friend here yet? We can come back later. Let's go get something to eat." He wraps his arm around my shoulders, and I let him lead me away.

By the time we return to my parents' apartment, the sky is turning from black to blue. George stumbles to his room and immediately falls into a heavy, snoring sleep, and I rush to the bathroom to change into my pajamas before my mother wakes up. But even when I've stuffed the black dress to the bottom of my duffel, I still feel anxious and dirty. I scrub my face and hands, but the smell of sweat and cigarette smoke sticks to my skin; the taste of stale beer lingers in my mouth. I can't sleep. When my mother comes out to make breakfast and finds me sitting on the sofa clutching my knees, she nods sadly and says, "You're ready to leave again."

"I'll come back," I tell her.

"I hope so."

I dress and get ready to go. My mother insists on doing my head wrap for me. I sit in front of the mirror and she smoothes my hair back from my forehead and pulls the fabric of the *gele* around the back of my head so that she is holding the two long ends in front of me. In that cradle of cloth, my head suddenly feels lighter, my neck loose and limp. She wraps the fabric across my forehead and pins it in place while she gathers the rest into her hands.

"I wish I could come home for good," I say.

"We all wish that. You come whenever you're ready." She lays her hand against the back of my neck. Her skin is cool and soft against mine. She finishes pleating the *gele* and fans the folds carefully above my head. Then she takes a handkerchief from her pocket to wipe my face. "Don't cry," she says. "I'm proud of you. How many girls could survive what you have?"

As she says it, I wonder if it's true, if I have survived. Until today, I have never missed my old self, the self that could be abducted, bullied, raped, made to marry a man for whom I had no feelings but dread and hatred. I have rejoiced many times in the death of that girl, but now my mother looks at me in the mirror and I know that's who she is looking for. I can feel it in the way her eyes sweep across my face.

Abike and I ride home in the back of a millet truck. For most of the ride she is silent, but I can tell she is watching me when my eyes are closed. When we are almost home, she reaches out tentatively and takes my hand.

I press my thumb against hers. "I'm not angry at you.

You didn't know," I say. We have reached our town, and I call for the driver to stop. Abike kisses my cheek. "I'm going to ride on to the market," she says. "I'll be home soon." I nod and don't look back as the truck pulls away.

The village is dusty and quiet. Stray dogs nap in the sun outside our house. When I go inside, Karim is at the stove, boiling water. He looks frightened when he sees me but tries to hide it. He pours two cups of tea and motions for me to sit down at the table.

"Go ahead," I say, and he sits across from me, resting his hands on the tabletop. The backs of his hands are dotted with the scars of old cigarette burns. For a while, this was something Abike and I liked to do. We could make him sit with his palms flat on the table while we pushed the lit end of the cigarette against his flesh. All his fear and pain would go across his face, but he wouldn't move his hands until we let him.

Now I look at Karim in a way I haven't looked at him in years, with no command in mind. For so long, he has been nothing to me but a curse I broke, a monster I hollowed out and made weak, but now it occurs to me how little I know about him: what his family is like, what he himself was like as a boy, how he came to be part of a band of ruthless men with guns. Whether he really believed in the Prophet or whether he just wanted three meals a day and something to do. His skin is bagged under the eyes, his hair patchy where he has worn it away with nervous scratching. He is only thirty-five years old. "Go and get Bashir," I tell him.

A few minutes later they return and sit side by side across the table from me.

"Bashir," I say, "my husband is going to divorce me. You are our witness. Karim, tell me that you are divorcing me."

He does it, without hesitation. To him this is no different from any other command, not freighted with meaning or emotion. He might as well be ordering food in a restaurant.

"Again," I tell him. "Again." And then it's over. He's not my husband anymore, he's just a man on the other side of a table. He sits quietly, watching me, waiting to hear what I'll say next. "I want you to leave. Go away from here," I tell him. "Never touch another woman as long as you live. If you do, you'll fall to your knees and never get up. Remember that." Even as I say it, I don't know if this is enough, if a man like this can ever be punished enough. But I am tired of being the one to punish him.

"Where do I go?" Karim says.

"Where do you want to go?"

He shrugs his shoulders weakly, but he doesn't look away. His gaze is the soft, searching gaze of a dog being scolded for a crime it doesn't understand. He waits for me to tell him what I want, what to do. What comes next.

And who knows the answer to that?

ROBERT GREENMAN AND
THE MERMAID

In Portsmouth, New Hampshire, there lived a fisherman named Robert Greenman. He was the latest in a long line of fishermen, thirty-three years old, quiet and ruggedly built just as his father had been. He had a pretty wife, Carol, a nurse he'd met at Portsmouth Regional Hospital when a cut on his arm had threatened to turn gangrenous. Sometimes when they lay in bed at night she liked to run her fingers along the scar that cut had made. They had been married a year and, so far, had no children, though certainly not for lack of trying, she liked to say, with a little laugh like wind chimes. Robert was, above all else, a sensible and sober man, and he adored Carol as only such a man could, with a love built on a list of reasons and proofs of her goodness. She was a charming woman, cheerful and intelligent, with strawberry-blond hair that she kept cut short, just below her ears. For work she wore sneakers and scrubs, but at home she favored dresses that showed her shoulders, and shoes with low heels that made a particular clicking noise that had become, in Robert's mind, the signature sound of women.

Now Carol was standing at the end of the Portsmouth dock in her bright blue wool coat, waving at Robert as his ship headed out to sea. He didn't wave back, he never did, but he knew that she didn't mind and wanted to wave anyway.

He was on board the *Ushuaia,* a cod-fishing ship headed up toward Newfoundland. The captain, known in Portsmouth simply as Tomás because his last name was considered unpronounceable, was an Argentine who had moved to New Hampshire when he was a young man. Robert had worked for Tomás before and liked him. The trip would last five weeks, if it took that long to fill the hold, and it probably would. Over the past several years, fishing along the New England coast had dwindled—the result of overfishing in previous decades—so that every season the captains had to push their crews out farther to make a profit. Robert had spent most of the year since his marriage at home with Carol, working odd jobs in town to supplement the money she made from nursing, but lately he had been going to sea again. He knew most of the crew on this trip. They had been fishing as long as he had, if not longer. The only person he did not know was Mark Leslie, who was new to town and, from the look of him, to fishing as well. Mark was pale, with limp blond hair and brown eyes that seemed too large for his face, like a child's. He was thirty years old but acted much younger. As the ship moved out into the bay, leaving Portsmouth, Mark leaned against the rail and stared down into the water, then turned and grinned at the other men on deck as though the mere sight of the ocean were something astounding.

The first night at sea was clear and warm. The fishermen sat on deck, talking and smoking. Mark pointed out the constellations, not just Orion and the Big Dipper and the ones they all knew, but others as well, the strange Greek names sliding easily off his tongue. When he finally stopped talking there was an awkward silence until the captain told a joke, and Jim Barner—the cook, and a friend of Robert's from high school—started laughing his high, shrill laugh that made him sound like a teenage girl. The other men began laughing and telling jokes as well. Robert chuckled and nodded along but he was watching Mark, who sat across from him on the other side of the circle of men. There was a thin line on a fishing ship between men who were useless and those whose incompetence endangered their shipmates; it was still unclear where Mark would fall.

Their target fishing ground was five days northward, a swath of ocean around the 55th parallel, just outside the bounds of Canadian fishing laws. As they traveled they worked, rechecking the nets, making sure that the ice machine in the hold was in working order to preserve the fish they would catch. On the fifth day, an hour before sunset, the captain looked up from the sonar and said there were fish around. He sent Robert and Mark to pay out the nets, and the motors of the net drums growled as they slowly unwound twenty miles' worth of woven monofilament line that would float through the water like a spider's web, reaching hungrily for the passing fish. They would let it drift with the tides and haul it in the following morning, to see what their fortune would be for this trip.

By the time they finished with the nets, the rest of the men were asleep. Robert felt his way through the dim bunkroom, and heard Mark stumble in behind him. They both got into their bunks, but as soon as Robert lay down he could tell this was one of those nights when he'd struggle with the insomnia that sometimes came over him at sea. He stayed in bed for an hour anyway, listening to the other men's breathing as they sank into heavy sleep. Then he donned his boots and jacket and went up on deck.

The moon had come out, and the waves were black, edged with foam and shivering streaks of light. Robert leaned against the rail, eyes drifting aimlessly over the waves, getting lost in their pattern. Then he saw the mermaid.

At first he thought she was a large fish breaching the surface. He saw only her tail as it slid beneath the waves, silver and glittering in the faint light from the moon. But even the sight of the tail tugged at his nerves. She surfaced again, and the nervousness hardened into a knot. Her skin was pearly white, and gave off the kind of glow he'd seen in certain jellyfish. She was perhaps forty feet from the ship, and she floated at the surface of the water with her tail submerged, facing away from him. A line of silver scales marked her spine and disappeared into her hair. She slipped in and out of the water, her tail propelling her quickly, gracefully, its movement delicate. She seemed to be looking for something, turning her head side to side, and every time she turned, he hoped to catch a glimpse of her face, but never saw more than a thin crescent of her profile. As he watched her, an ache filled his bones. The light from her skin made everything around her dull. The moon-capped waves, the stars, even the black water lost their gloss. Eventually, she dove underneath the waves and didn't reappear. Robert watched for her until the sun came up, and when the other men shuffled onto deck, yawning, he joined them.

They pulled in the nets and Robert scanned the deck, afraid that he would spot a pair of white arms among the lines, but he saw only fish. It was a fair catch, nothing to brag about, but enough to put a little money in each of their pockets. Robert loaded fish into the hold. He was not superstitious, as many fishermen were. His eyes and ears did not play tricks on him and he was not given to daydreaming under any circumstances; certainly not while on board a ship, where so many things could go wrong. He trusted himself completely. So the mermaid must be real. He wondered only where she had gone when she disappeared.

...

The mermaid had been born at the bottom of the ocean, a place beyond the reach of sunlight, warmed only by the muttering of geothermal vents. She had wandered up out of those depths and spent her early years on the slopes of an underwater mountain near the tiny islands of Tristan da Cunha, thirteen hundred miles from the next piece of dry land. Every memory from the moment sunlight had touched her eyes was clear, frozen, perfectly preserved even decades later, but of her birthplace she retained only a vague impression of magnificent creatures with skin like a carpet of teeth, of tentacles that snapped and plucked blindfish from the water, and currents that burst from the lips of the vents like magma, warmth from the very core of the earth. Among these hazy memories there was no picture of another mermaid.

Eventually she had followed a swordfish north, along the coast of South America, and then up to Newfoundland. The water, as she traveled, turned from sapphire blue to a murky gray-green, and the fish grew larger but lost their bright colors. She did not find the northern seas as appealing as those she was used to, but she was a creature of endless curiosity. Still, she might have turned around and gone back to warmer waters were it not for the shark.

He was hard to see, even when he was moving. He blended so completely with the deep sea that he could have been a shadow, a swell of agitated water, a cloud of black sand sent up by a manta ray. The mermaid observed him from a distance, watching for the white flash of his belly whenever he twisted to change direction.

She had decided it was best to approach him when he had just eaten. Not that he ever made any move to attack her—he preferred to surprise his prey, and the mermaid was watchful. But he was calmer after eating. When he was hungry, the shark dove deep into the water until he was invisible from above. As she waited for him to resurface, the mermaid felt a strange electric trill at the back of her neck. She became suddenly aware of the water against her skin, something she seldom otherwise noticed. The shark circled slowly until he had spotted his prey, and then he shot upward, mouth open, sometimes bursting above the surface of the ocean with his attack. After gorging himself, he swam in lazy circles while blood still clouded the water.

The mermaid began to search for fish, finding the biggest ones in the surrounding ocean, corralling them toward him. She experimented first with a snapper, slashing a piece of sharpened shell against its side. The fish jerked away from her with a powerful flip of its tail, but a stream of blood trailed behind it. She kept the snapper in sight, and waited.

The shark could smell blood miles away, could feel the telltale vibrations in the water that a wounded fish made. He charged up from below in an explosion of turbulence, bit the snapper in half and swallowed it in two bites. When he had finished eating, the mermaid swam cautiously toward him. His flat, black eyes followed her, but he did not seem disturbed, and she edged closer and pressed her hands against his side. His skin was rough, covered with serrations too small to see, and his blood beneath it was not the cold blood of a fish; it was as warm as her own. Touching that skin thrilled the mermaid, propagated broods of memories that skittered through the depths of her mind. The shark was a solid whip of muscle, carelessly lethal, and his presence transformed the drab green of the northern sea into a place she longed for even though she could not properly recall it. He dove deeper, the water changed from green to gray to nearly black, and eventually the mermaid left him and spiraled away on her own.

She swam to a spot she especially liked, a large chunk of volcanic rock that rested on the seafloor, worn smooth by years of tides and sand. The mermaid sank down into a hollow of it and began to sing. Her voice had a deep, liquid sound like a separate current within the water. The shark could hear it but it meant nothing to him, and he paid no attention to it. The fish heard it, too, though, and they were entranced by it. The song was the sound of joy without depth, of clear waters and warm blood and the sunlight that pierced the tops of the waves. Fish were drawn from miles away. They orbited the mermaid in a slow swirl of fins and scales, and she could think only that the shark would be well fed, that she could be close to him more often.

When Robert arrived back at port, twenty-nine days after setting out, Carol was standing at the end of the dock waiting, as though she had not moved during that entire month. In the parking lot, she hugged him tightly. He kissed the top of her head and tried to find the scent of her hair beneath the smell of disinfectant and the sickly sweet air freshener they used at the hospital.

"Was it a good trip?" she asked, as they got into their car.

Robert thought about the mermaid, and knew he wouldn't tell Carol about her.

"Not a bad catch. Nothing spectacular, though. It won't be much money," he said.

"Did you miss me?"

"Of course," he said, but realized he hadn't.

Usually, like all the fishermen, Robert enjoyed being back on land after a long trip, but now he felt restless. Sometimes he found himself, in the middle of one of Carol's stories about the hospital, ignoring her words and thinking that her voice had a shrill edge to it. He wondered why he had not noticed it before. He began looking for projects to keep himself busy, cleaning out the attic and the basement, re-painting the toolshed. He did not know how to doubt himself, which would have been the easiest thing to do, and so he was forced to try to live his life as though steady work and a watertight roof and a loving wife were still as impor-tant as they had been before he had seen the mermaid.

Robert started spending time at the Lock and Dock, the local fishermen's bar. It was a place he usually avoided, tell-ing Carol he'd seen more than enough of his friends during their time at sea. Now he went frequently and the talk was always about the same thing. No one was catching. Men on land-leave drank all night, running up tabs they couldn't pay, and fights were frequent. Some of these men had been to sea on and off for a year without ever being home for more than a few weeks at a time, trying to find the catch that would give them money for their car payments, their mortgages, for the debts they had accumulated back when fish were plentiful. Robert realized that the crew of the *Ushuaia* hadn't fared too badly with their mediocre catch; most trips weren't even making back their expenses.

He often saw Mark Leslie at the bar, sitting alone in a corner booth. One night, against his better judgment, Robert joined him. Mark was reading a book, which he politely put down when Robert approached. They made small talk for a few minutes, until Mark said, "So, will you be going on the next trip?"

"Will you?" said Robert, surprised. They'd hit a train of small storms on the way back to Portsmouth, and Mark had spent most of the return trip throwing up over the side of the boat.

Mark nodded. "Tomás said he'd take me on as an apprentice if I was willing to work without pay for a few trips. He and my grandfather were friends, back when Tomás was just starting out. And I've always loved the sea."

Robert looked down at his beer to avoid frowning directly at Mark. Taking on a man with no experience, whether he was free labor or not, was irresponsible. Mark had a romantic's vision of the sea, which was nothing like the under-standing of men who earned their living by it. During the last journey he had made a fool of himself, and of the other men, by asking ridiculous questions: What was the best time of year to watch the sunset? What did native legends say about this part of the sea? Were there any endangered species in the area? They did not know the answers, al-though they had been fishing Great Bay since they were teenagers. These things did not matter to them. Robert gulped the rest of his beer and said his goodbyes.

The next afternoon, when Robert came back from the hard-ware store, Carol said that Tomás had called, that he was planning to head for Newfoundland again in two weeks, and had asked if Robert would ship out with him. Robert nod-ded, and let out a slow sigh that belied the nervous quiver-ing in his stomach. Carol, still wearing her scrubs, sat down beside him on the couch.

"You just got here," she said.

"I'll be back soon. Maybe with some real money this time."

"I could just work an extra shift or two. We're doing all right."

Robert put one hand against the back of her neck. He wanted to see the mermaid again, and he did not. He rubbed the ends of Carol's hair between his fingers.

"It won't be too long," he said.

...

There were high winds the day the *Ushuaia* left Portsmouth, but when it reached the spot that had provided its meager bounty the last time, the ocean was calm.

For a week, Robert spent his evenings watching for the mermaid while the other men drank and played cards, but he did not see her. Finally, one night when everyone else was asleep, he stole up onto deck and unlashed the lifeboat that was tied to the edge of the ship. Climbing inside, he lowered it into the water with the ropes and pulleys. He took the oars from the side of the lifeboat and began to row until he was about five hundred feet from the ship. With every pull of the oars, he felt increasingly uneasy. The waves were larger than they had looked from the deck of the *Ushuaia*, and the sound and smell of them was inescapable. For all his years at sea, he had spent precious little time this close to the water, and there was good reason for it. The ocean here was a mile or more deep; if they were to move a few miles farther eastward they would be over the edge of the continental shelf, and the water would reach down forever into bottomless trenches of blackness. He tried to put those depths out of his mind as he brought the oars in and looked over the edge of the boat. He thought about calling out, but realized it would be useless. If the mermaid were on the surface and near enough to hear him, he would see her—with that luminous skin—and if she wasn't, she wouldn't hear him through the waves. He dragged his fingers slowly through the water, imagining for a moment that he could feel the plankton in it, all the thousands of invisible creatures that float on the surface of the sea. Then he saw a faint white glow beneath the waves several feet away, coming closer, and he pulled his hand back quickly as though it had been burned, holding it against his chest.

The mermaid rose to the surface and hooked her long, pale fingers over the edge of the boat. Now that she was close enough to touch, Robert still could not say if she was beautiful. She had large, wide-set eyes, dark green in color. Her lashless eyelids were translucent. He would have said her hair was tangled except that it did not look as though it should be otherwise; he felt that combing it out would be like trying to comb a person's limbs. Each indigo strand was as thick as a twig, and had the moist look of an anemone. All her veins were clearly visible beneath her skin. Her breasts were small, and he realized this would be necessary, that her whole body must be streamlined for moving through the ocean. She had a wide mouth, with lips the color of seawater. He could not see, through the tangle of hair, whether she had ears. Her nose was thin and her fingers were webbed with the same tissue that made up her eyelids, flesh that looked delicate but that must be incredibly strong.

He reached out slowly and touched her arm. She flinched but did not move away. Her skin was cool and moist. Robert felt as though the tips of his fingers where he touched her were dissolving.

He stripped off his clothes and lowered himself into the water. The chill cut through his skin instantly. He hadn't actually been in the ocean in years, although he was used to being drenched in spray or rain while he was on the ship. He was a strong swimmer, but the cold was debilitating. Forcing himself to let go of the edge of the lifeboat, he reached for the mermaid. She stayed afloat easily, flicking her tail back and forth beneath the surface of the ocean, and did not move away when he placed his hands on her shoulders. He ran his fingertips tentatively over her collarbone, her face, through her hair, and below the water her tail fins stroked his legs, caressing his feet and toes as nimbly as fingers would, and sending a crackle like static shock through his skin. The feeling the mermaid inspired in Robert was not lust, or love, or curiosity; it was a feeling he did not recall having before, a sense of wonder that traveled with his blood and invaded every part of his body. While he was touching her, the rest of the world faded from his notice, and it was only when she ducked beneath the water that he saw that the lifeboat had drifted a hundred feet away. If his muscles cramped, which seemed increasingly likely in the frigid water, he would never make it back. He could see the mermaid below him in the water and lunged for her, but she dodged him. When he surfaced, he turned reluctantly away and swam to the lifeboat.

As he pulled himself over the side, his leg muscles began to spasm, and he fell into the bottom of the boat. He grabbed his T-shirt and used it to dry himself as well as he could, then struggled into his sweater. He pulled on his pants and rowed back to the *Ushuaia*, pulling hard, his arm muscles threatening to seize up. By the time he managed to climb on board and haul the lifeboat up, he was shivering uncontrollably, and the sky was beginning to lighten.

When everyone had had their breakfast and assembled on deck with the hooks they used to move the fish, Jim Barner began to draw in the catch. The net rose, foot by foot, and Jim closed his eyes and listened to the sound of the motors. A moment later, the first fish came into view.

There were more fish than Robert had seen in years. The net was heavy with them, the monofilament lines straining to hold them. The men all stood blinking for a moment, then grinned at one another. Jim whooped like a cowboy and moved swiftly to the controls that would bring the fish on board.

The crew spent the rest of the day putting fish into the hold and cleaning the deck. In addition to cod, they had caught a few tuna, some snapper. Those that were still alive thrashed around the deck, trying to make their way back to the water, their slick scales turning dull in the sun. There was a dolphin, too, and Mark Leslie was distraught when he saw it, dropping his hook, running over to it and throwing his arms around the animal as though it were his sister.

"Just look at it," Mark said. "It's practically human. Look at the *eyes*." He struggled with the dolphin until Robert came to help him and they heaved the animal back over the rail into the water. Mark stood and watched it swim away with a look somewhere between awe and grief, and Robert had the feeling that Mark would have called a goodbye to it, if he hadn't known the other men would ridicule him for it.

That night, Jim Barner cooked a feast in the galley. Robert sat among the crew trying to look pleased with himself, but he could feel the emptiness of his smile. He was light-headed with exhaustion and yet, when the other men finally finished drinking and went to bed, he found that, again, he could not sleep. The world shifted around him in patches of gray fluorescence, every sound in the bunkroom was magnified, and a dull buzz began building at the back of his skull. Eventually he went to the deck. He watched until sunup, but did not see the mermaid.

The mermaid was ecstatic. Her shark had more food than he needed; he glutted himself, and after every feeding the mermaid circled around him and sang. As weeks passed, her melody gained a deeper resonance, reverberated along the great ridge that marks the spine of the Atlantic and spread farther. She called fish from the deep sea, swordfish and bass, whole schools of mackerel. And others, fish that had never before ventured north: angelfish, clown fish, spotted eels. A school of orange-and-pink parrot fish followed the sound of her voice from the balmy waters off Florida up toward the north seas, their body temperatures plummeting as they went, until they died suddenly, as a group, and rose to the surface of the ocean in a multicolored cloud. The fish that followed the mermaid's song ignored migratory patterns, potential prey, and the baited lines of the trawling boats; they thought of nothing but moving north toward her.

On the *Ushuaia* the catches were good every day, so good that the fishermen began to feel uncomfortable about it. This kind of abundance hadn't been seen since most of them were children, if ever. One day, Robert walked to the bow and found the captain staring down into the water.

"I can see them," Tomás said. "I swear I can."

Robert looked and, through the glow of the sun on the waves, he thought he, too, saw shifting layers of movement just below the surface, as though the ocean were so full of fish it was preparing to overflow.

It took them two weeks to fill the hold, and in that time Robert slept no more than a few hours each night. For the most part, everyone else was too busy hauling fish and getting drunk to notice, but he thought Mark Leslie looked at him strangely sometimes as they passed in the hall between the galley and bunks. Robert saw the mermaid every night. He had found an old wet suit in the storage room and now lowered himself with a rope that he dropped from the prow of the ship, straight into the water. The suit gave him an extra layer of protection, but his arms and his legs below the knees were still exposed, and going into the ocean inevitably left him drained, weak, shivering. Still, he wanted to be as close to the mermaid as he could. The chill of the water faded into obscurity when her moist, searching fingers were trailing along his calves. She was fascinated by his legs, spent long minutes wrapping her arms around them, every touch sending painful pulses of electricity through his body. He stayed beside her until he could feel hypothermia edging in and, against the pull of his desire, forced himself to leave the water.

Robert could not say that he enjoyed being with the mermaid, just that she was the only thing that seemed to be real. The phosphorescence of her skin, the silver reflections of her tail were more tangible than the ocean or the ship or the food he ate every day. The sparks of energy that went through his hands or face when she touched them were the only sensations that fully pierced the veil of exhaustion and lethargy that had settled over the rest of his life. He got so little sleep, he sometimes thought it would kill him.

When the hold was full, they went home. They were days ahead of schedule, but Carol had somehow heard and was there waiting for him on the dock. She took his face in her hands and kissed him. Her body seemed to have very little weight or scent, and she looked paler than usual.

"Are you feeling all right?" he asked.

"The house gets lonely without you," she said. "There's nobody to get dock grease all over my hand towels and keep me up at night with his snoring."

Robert leaned against the car, looking toward the docks although he couldn't see the ocean from the parking lot, listening for the sound of the water.

"I'm joking," Carol said.

"What?"

"I'm glad you're back."

He nodded, and let her hug him again, opening the door for her so she could get in the car and take him home.

That night the crew of the *Ushuaia*, all of them but Robert, made their way to the Lock and Dock to celebrate their success. They were bursting with money and good will when they entered the bar, but their exuberance quickly faded under the jealous stares of the other fishermen. While the *Ushuaia* had been hauling in thousands of dollars a day, no one else's luck had changed. The faces around the bar were still grim. The crew gathered at a corner table and quietly toasted their luck until they had drunk enough that they forgot to be quiet. Then they started singing, endless choruses of misremembered lyrics. When Tomás heard about it the next day, he called every one of them and told them that if they wanted to have another good haul and another payout in a few weeks, they had better stay quiet and keep their money low.

Robert Greenman found himself finally ready to sleep. Over the course of the next week he slept twelve, fourteen, eighteen hours a day. He dreamed of monsters from the deep, jagged teeth and wide-open jaws, suction cups as big as tires adhering to his chest and back. He moved through ranges of underwater mountains covered in waving seaweed, a place both terrifying and alluring, while the shadows of massive fish passed over him.

When he was awake, the world was drab. The buzz of

insomnia in the back of his head had relented, but Carol's
voice took its place, so that she always seemed to be speaking to him from far away. He found that if he concentrated,
everything she said made sense, that her voice was the same
pleasant, soothing voice she had always had. But it was an
effort to perceive her this way, and when he didn't bother
she seemed strange—her movements awkward, her features too sharp, her eyes small and dim.

All he could think about was getting back to sea, but
Carol did her best to divert him. She began planning trips
for them on her days off, to the movies, to new restaurants
they had to drive three towns over to get to. She invited
friends he hadn't seen in years over for dinner, and when he
dragged himself out of bed at noon, the house was already
filled with the scent of sautéed onions or chopped herbs,
smells he found cloying.

One Sunday morning Robert woke to find Carol shaking
him gently as pale sunlight poured over her shoulders, leaving her face in shadow and making him squint.

"Get up, we're going shopping," she said.

"Go without me."

"I need your opinion."

"We don't need anything anyway."

"You've brought home more money than we know what
to do with," she said. "What's the point in making all this
money if we can't spend it? Get up."

He dressed, drank a glass of water for breakfast, and

slumped against the window in the car as Carol drove. He wanted nothing more than to go back to sleep, but there was such a crispness about Carol's actions, the way she wrapped her fingers around the steering wheel and held her head, that they didn't seem to brook any disagreement. It reminded him of how she had acted when he was her patient—firm and capable, radiating assurance.

When they reached the mall, Carol walked up and down between rows of overstuffed leather sofas that reminded Robert of great overfed cows, not the kind of thing Carol would buy at all, and he wondered why she was even looking at them. She led him through a department store, examining pots and pans, rubbing bath towels against her face to check their softness. Eventually she found the sporting goods section, where she picked up a cheap rod-and-reel set and examined it minutely, as though it held secrets in its plastic casing.

"We should go fishing together," she said. "We could go out to that lake by Wamset."

"Lake fishing is just waiting with a pole in your hand," said Robert.

"Well I guess I've gotten pretty good at waiting," she said. "And I think it would be fun."

She tucked the rod under her arm and began looking at bait, fingering through tubs of sparkling green rubber worms that only a thirty-pounder could swallow, peering into jars of cinnamon-red salmon eggs as though selecting expensive produce. She chose a jar and shook it, then held it up along with the handful of worm lures and said, "Which one?"

Robert envied her for a moment, her ability to focus so intensely on trivial things as though they were important. He knew that, once, cleaning gutters, hauling fish, and admiring the fine curve of Carol's neck had been substantial material to fill the days of his life, and that it had all dissolved now into sea-foam, a puff of nothing. Carol would go along happily forever, he thought, and just then she put the jar back on the shelf and said, "Are you sorry you married me?"

"What?"

"I don't like you being gone all the time, but I could stand it if you were different when you came home. You don't even talk to me anymore."

"I'm talking to you right now."

"Don't play dumb, Robert," she said, her voice rising.

"We're in a store. Don't yell."

"Who cares? Do we know these people? I'm worried about you."

"I'm fine," he said, but he knew it wasn't true. Many things had been wrong lately. He had trouble concentrating, and his bedsheets seemed to scratch his skin when he pulled them up at night. The people he passed in the street all looked as though they had contracted a disease; they were slow, squint-eyed, their skin the color of dishwater.

"Then why are you acting this way?" she said.

"Maybe I haven't been feeling quite well."

"Well, why don't you say so?" she said, crying now and wiping her face with the back of her hand. "You can't just walk around sick all the time, and you're scaring me. I want you to talk to one of the doctors at the hospital."

A doctor would not be able to do anything, he thought. A doctor would not even begin to understand. "All right," he said.

He looked down at the bucket of sparkling rubber worms, thought of the creatures of his dreams, the glimmers of phosphorescent life that were teeming through deep waters somewhere every minute of the day, unseen, even now. He thought of the glimmer of a silver tail, skin like mother-of-pearl.

"Promise?" said Carol.

He squeezed his eyes shut. What had he promised? When he opened them again, Carol was staring at him, her eyes rimmed pink, lips taut with unhappiness.

"Yes, yes, I do," he said, and she sniffed and pressed her warm, wet face against his chest.

The doctor she sent him to prescribed an antidepressant, and told Carol to keep Robert off the boats for a while. So the *Ushuaia* sailed without him, and he sat at the end of the dock and watched it go.

The antidepressants gave the world a different sort of unreality where everything was excessively bright, where he found he could not stop talking even though he was not a talkative man. For the next three weeks, he spent most of his waking hours at the Lock and Dock and returned home every night exhausted. Carol pulled him into bed, made love to him desperately, and, as soon as they were finished, he was asleep. His dreams were more vivid than ever, and their images spilled over into his waking hours. When the *Ushuaia* came back into port with another full hold, he told Carol he was going on the next trip no matter what.

She argued with him and finally refused to drive him to the dock when the departure day arrived. Robert was so close to being back at sea that he was nearly twitching with anticipation, but he forced himself to stay in bed with her until the last possible moment; to hold her; to wipe the tears off her face and tell her that he loved her, that he would be back soon. He called for a taxi, boarded the ship with his duffel bag, and began helping with the final preparations for castoff. As the *Ushuaia* was pulling away from the dock, he caught sight of Carol on the pier, half-hidden behind one of the pilings, trying not to let him see her, and he waved.

There was heavy rain when they got to the fishing ground off Newfoundland, and the possibility of a storm, so they didn't let the nets out right away. The crew members spent their time huddled in the cabins smoking, but their spirits were high. They were certain another hold full of fish awaited them as soon as the weather abated. Robert sat on his bunk in the midst of the chatter and curling smoke and tried not to fidget. Eventually he put on his rain slicker and went out on deck, instantly feeling much calmer. A moment later, Mark Leslie was standing beside him, holding tight to the rail and looking as though he might vomit.

"Get back below," Robert said. "You'll get soaked."

"I saw her," said Mark.

Robert tried his best not to let his expression change, to tell himself that he was jumping to conclusions. He said nothing.

"All those nights you came in late, I knew you were up to something," Mark said. "Smuggling, I thought. I even followed you once, but you were just standing, looking at the water. So on the last trip I went up there every night and stood in your place, trying to see what you saw. There was nothing and I thought, maybe it's just the ocean. He wants to look at the ocean. But then I saw her. She was swimming with that *thing*."

"What thing?" asked Robert.

Mark's eyes became sly, veiled in possessiveness. "I wondered whether you knew, but no? No."

Such a stab of bitter loathing passed through Robert that he turned away. The clouded sky had made the sea truly dark, as no place on land could ever be. He could hear the patter of raindrops against the waves forming a sweet, clear slick of fresh water on the ocean's surface. Mark was still talking, but Robert shut his ears against it, until Mark said, "It was the biggest shark I've ever seen. Twenty feet long and swimming past the side of the ship, and she was right behind it."

Robert tried to picture this, to cast the image onto the black waves below them, the pure white-and-silver body of the mermaid pursuing the grim bulk of the shark. "Hunting it?" said Robert.

"No. She couldn't. If it wanted to, it could destroy her in one bite, it's that monstrous. I don't think it even knew she was there." Mark was sopping now, his fair hair dark with water and sleek against his skull, rain dripping from his chin and nose. "You weren't going to tell anyone, were you? I mean, of course you weren't. Who would even believe us?"

Robert shook his head. He didn't care for Mark's moist-eyed reverence, and yet he saw that Mark took naturally to the mermaid, to the intrusion of such implausibility into his life. That he had, in fact, been waiting for just such a thing to happen to him, and so its coming to pass could not harm him. Robert turned to leave, but Mark grabbed his arm.

"Tell me something about her," Mark said. "You must know something, you've known about her for months. Does she talk to you?" Robert stared at him, tight-lipped, wordless, wondering what would happen if he simply punched Mark in the mouth, but Mark held tight. "I want to touch her," he said.

Robert avoided Mark after that, as much as it was possible to avoid someone within the confines of a ship. The thought of the shark troubled Robert, but it bothered him at least as much to think that Mark might know something about the mermaid that he, Robert, did not. Robert spent every night pacing the deck. Mercifully, Mark did not have Robert's capacity for sleep deprivation, and after working a sixteen-hour day was often too tired to last the night, whatever his intentions might have been. When Robert finally saw the mermaid and the shark, he was alone.

The shark was cutting through the very top of the water, its dorsal fin exposed. The mermaid held on to the fin, and pressed her body against the shark's. Robert watched. And then he began to yell at her, to scream like a madman, waving his arms to get her attention. She did not respond; he had decided she couldn't hear sounds that were airborne, but that didn't stop him from screaming. Finally, she glanced up, by chance, and saw him, but as quickly as her eyes registered him, she looked away again. He watched her and the shark trace the edge of the ship, and her expression was one of pure delight. It made her face beautiful, and it was nothing like the look of searching curiosity he saw when she stroked his legs. He stood at the rail, watching them, until the shark dove underwater and the mermaid followed.

In the morning, the crew of the *Ushuaia* hauled up the nets, and the net drums creaked in a way they had all become familiar with. The men stood around, grinning, shifting on their feet with anticipation, thinking that by the end of the day they would have moved several thousand dollars' worth of fish into the hold. But when the nets were up and the fish spilled onto the deck, the crew stood still and quiet. There were no cod, or mackerel, or swordfish. The fish they had caught were lemon yellow, magenta, electric blue. They were striped and spotted, fish the crew had never seen before outside of photographs, fish that had no business being in the northern Atlantic. They covered the deck like a brightly colored quilt, and the sound of their bodies slapping against the deck filled the men's silence. Too many fish was something they could rejoice in. They could ignore the fact that it made no sense, could believe that God had created a special fountain of fish off the coast of Newfoundland just for them. But this was unnatural. The rainbow fish were unsettling and aberrant beneath the gray sky. Jim Barner nudged one with his toe, a two-foot-long yellow fish that had a blue crest and a blue ring around its eye and little puckered lips that made it look like it wanted a kiss. The fish's gills flared halfheartedly, and Jim bent down and grabbed it and flung it over the rail.

"What did we do?" said Tomás.

"Help me," said Jim, and he picked up another fish and threw it back.

They worked at it all day. Most of the fish were dead by the time they got back in the water; they littered the sea around the *Ushuaia* like confetti. Robert worked along with the rest of the crew, although less frantically. He kept thinking about the mermaid and the shark, wondering if he would see her again. He thought at first that he would not dare go back into the water with her, knowing that the shark might be close behind, but he realized he would go anyway, that he would brave the shark the same way he had braved the cold, and all for a creature who found him nothing more than a curious diversion. Because she was still as entrancing as she had been all these months, even if he meant nothing to her.

Every night the fishermen sent the nets out, and every morning they brought in another net full of strange fish. They did not bring them on board anymore, but simply lowered the net again, dumping them back into the ocean. The men began to tell Tomás that the place had become cursed, that they should turn back, but the captain could not settle with the idea of returning to Portsmouth empty-handed. So they kept at it, and two weeks passed without a single fish being put into the hold.

Robert watched for the mermaid by night, but did not see her. He knew she had brought the tropical fish, although he couldn't say how. He wondered where she was, what she was doing. After seven days and six nights of watching, he finally slept through the night.

When he woke, the bunkroom was empty. He dressed quickly and headed for the deck. The sky at the top of the hold was a block of bright cloudless blue that grew as he approached it. He heard the other men laughing and talking, and realized this was a sound he had not heard for days; grim silence had become the usual state of the ship.

On deck the men were gathered around Mark Leslie, slapping him on the back, all of them drinking beers while Mark grinned idiotically. Robert stepped farther out onto the deck and saw the shark. It was hanging by its tail, jaws open, two-inch teeth displayed in rows. They had measured it; it was not twenty feet, it was twenty-three. Even out of the water it was slick black, even dead it was terrifying. Robert walked up to it, past Mark and the men, and Mark sobered as soon as he saw Robert and turned to watch him. Robert reached into the shark's mouth, thinking that his entire torso would fit into that maw, and touched one of the teeth, pressing downward until the tip of it punctured his fingertip. A drop of bright blood appeared, and it glowed with color that the rest of the world lacked. Mark was standing behind him now, nervous and wheedling, all his drunken bravado gone.

"It would have killed her," Mark said. "I had to get rid of it. I threw some bait in the water and I got it with the harpoon gun. You should have seen it fight. I shot it right through the skull and it still kept going. I thought it was never going to die. I was scared stiff, even from up here."

Robert nodded. He turned to the rail and looked down at the water. There was no sign of the mermaid, but he knew she was there. Waves smacked against the side of the boat, and Robert thought he could feel their vibration in his hands, and with them another sound. He leaned closer to listen, and leaned farther, and then he was pitching over the rail, into the water below.

He was surrounded by the green of the seawater, and the water was full of a sound that made him feel as though he could start crying and never stop, as though his blood were turning to brine, as though the world were nothing but shades of gray. The mermaid was singing, and he knew from the song that she had seen the shark's body, and that she would not come back. She was going, but for the moment, the ocean, the salt that filled his mouth, the rush and swell of the waves, all of it was real, all of it was as vibrant and as painful as anything he had ever known. The song twisted through him, and the last tenuous line that moored him to what had been his life gave way. He was laid open, filled to overflowing. Then there was a splash beside him, and a thick arm around his waist, and he was pulled, struggling, from the water.

ANYTHING YOU MIGHT WANT

Every time Michael told Gina about how he had become her father's debtor—*the old man's slave,* he always said—the story changed a bit. He might linger over his description of the bar where he and the old man met, The Blue Mustang, painting for her the horseshoes nailed along the edge of the bar, the locked door leading to the back room with the illegal poker games, the fat beads of air jiggling up the tubes of the Wurlitzer during the twelve hours they played cards. Or he might, as he traced a finger along Gina's hairline, her lips, the edge of her collarbone, describe her father: the way the old man laughed even when he was losing, the way his eyes narrowed to slits when he looked at his cards, only once per hand, no double-checking no matter how high the stakes. Sometimes Michael skimmed over the whole night at The Blue Mustang and focused on better days, three straight weeks of a winning streak that had started on his twenty-sixth birthday and had taken him from Reno to Denver, leaving him feeling like he could turn any card to an ace just by brushing his fingers across it. But the story always ended the same way, back at the bar with him losing hand after hand, losing his temper and his money and digging himself deeper until he dug himself right down into Gina's father's coal mine, working ten-hour days to pay the old man back for all the bets made with money Michael didn't have. His hands, while he spoke, were always gentle, but his voice tightened like a guitar string.

"You know what he said to me on my first day? 'If you disappeared into one of those mine shafts, nobody would do a thing about it. Nobody would even notice. Think about that before you start making plans to sneak off in the middle of the night.'"

"He's not lying," Gina said. "He has cops in his pocket all over the state. But I'd notice." What she didn't say was that she had her own theory about how Michael had ended up in that bar.

Gina was eighteen and had never left Montana or even her hometown. She had a room full of designer clothes and jewelry and expensive shoes, and she hated it all. Her father would let her spend thousands of dollars on a horse she never bothered riding, but he wouldn't let her go to Billings with her friends for the weekend. He would pay a driver to take her around town, but he would not buy her a car, or even let her buy one herself. She had a job at the convenience store in town that she kept only so she could spend twenty hours a week somewhere she knew he wouldn't bother her, and the money from her paycheck just piled up waiting for some use she hadn't yet figured out.

Her older sisters, June and Laura, weren't smart enough to get away with anything, so they had solved their problems by marrying young and packing their new husbands off to Missoula. Once they were gone, it was harder for Gina to avoid her father's scrutiny. On nights she wasn't working and couldn't sneak away, she would lock herself in her room and lie in bed with the radio on, plotting her escape. She began to picture the man who would get her out of Montana. Not someone boring, like June and Laura's husbands. Not a husband at all. Someone exciting. Someone who hated Montana as much as she did.

When her father was drunk and in a lecturing mood, he loved to say, "If you really want something, you have to imagine every step of how you're going to get it, and then you take it without mercy." It was how he operated with everyone, and it was why half the people in town hated him, but Gina had to admit that maybe there was something to the philosophy, given that he owned everything in sight. So she imagined—the way the man who would be her escape would walk, and sound, and smile. The way he would drink a pop and zip his jeans. The kind of shoes he would wear and how he would smell in the heat of summer. She imagined him until she got to the point where every time she turned a street corner in town she expected to bump right into him.

The night Gina met Michael was one of her sisters' rare visits home; when their father headed out to the bar, Gina and Laura and June got into Laura's car and drove down to the lake. Laura and June were drunk on a shared six-pack and cackling with laughter. At the lakeside they left their dresses spread out like empty shells along the pebbled shore, slipped into the cool water, and made their way swiftly to the middle of the lake. They were all strong swimmers, and they spent an hour dipping between the dark water and the clear, sweet light of the moon.

When they swam back to the beach, they slicked the water off their bodies with their fingers, and Laura and June put on their dresses. Gina found her sandals but not her clothes; she walked across the beach, searching, but the night was windless, and until she heard a rustle in the bushes, followed by a quick burst of laughter, she couldn't imagine what could have happened to the dress. She walked toward the underbrush cursing, eyes boring into the darkness, and crashed through the branches to find a group of men blinking up at her, beer bottles littering the ground around them, and Michael waving her dress above his head like a trophy.

Gina didn't say anything, and she didn't try to cover herself. She stared into a dozen-odd pairs of glittering eyes and recognized, one by one, faces she sometimes saw coming out of the mine at closing time. The same realization came over the men, so that they dropped their gazes and shuffled backward into the shadows, muttering apologies. All except Michael, who stayed leaning against a pine tree, lazily grinning up at her while she stared at him. Eventually one of the other miners crawled up to him and whispered in his ear, and then the grin disappeared. Michael turned his face away, held the dress out to her, and, when she took it, got to his feet and ran. But already she wanted to run after him, to bring him back, to tell him she knew why he was there, even if he didn't.

After that, she noticed him everywhere: coming out of the movie theater; sprawled in the shade of the big oak trees in the park; sitting at the counter at the doughnut shop, licking powdered sugar off his fingers. He hunched over when he ate his breakfast, just like she had imagined he would. He had a tattoo snaking around his left biceps, the way he was supposed to. Every time she saw him she looked at him long and hard before she went back to what she was doing, and he blushed heavily and dropped his eyes.

When she found him sitting alone at Piper's Grill, two months after the night at the lake, she decided enough was enough. As always, he turned away from her, but she walked over to his booth and sat down across from him, taking half his grilled cheese sandwich from his plate.

"Do you work at my daddy's mine?" she said.

"Yes."

"Do you like it?"

He took a gulp of his drink and she watched him, biting the crisp corners off his sandwich and enjoying his discomfort.

"There are other places I'd rather be," he said finally.

"Damn right," she said. "Like *anywhere*."

He laughed, and so did she, but he didn't say anything else and looked down at his plate again.

"You've already seen me naked," Gina said. "Which most of the boys in this town would give their right eye for, by the way, so I don't see the point in getting shy at this late date."

"Could you keep your voice down? Your father would kill me."

"He'd kill both of us," she said, "and we haven't even done anything yet."

It wasn't hard to invent ways to cross paths in a town that small. At five-thirty, Gina would leave her house and walk to the Frosty Freeze, the only restaurant near the mine, and sit there drinking a pop with her bare feet up on the wooden rail of the porch until Michael walked by on his way home. Sometimes, if no one else was around, he would stop and exchange a few words with her, but other times he only blew gently against the soles of her feet as he passed. At night, he often came to the convenience store during her shift, just before closing, and spent long minutes browsing the magazine section until all the other customers were gone. As soon as the door closed behind the last patron, Gina would call out from the cash register, "Are you looking

for the porno magazines, sir? Because we keep those behind the counter. I'd be happy to show you our selection."
She liked the way he laughed, shaking his head as if he were
ashamed of her, walking toward her but still looking at the
floor.

Only once did he ever allow her into the rented room
where he lived, and then he pulled the curtains shut and
turned the TV up loud before he sat next to her on the narrow bed, as though spies might be lurking in the hallway,
ears pressed to the door. After a few minutes of nervous
conversation she sent him across the street to get beer, and
took the opportunity to quickly sift through his belongings.
The room was crammed with odds and ends that he collected from the curb: facsimile paintings in fake gilt frames,
ceramic lamps shaped like animals, furniture with six coats
of paint. In his dresser, underneath his socks, was a plastic
baggie of marijuana, which she had never seen him smoke,
and a stack of letters bound with a rubber band, the same
softly looped handwriting on each envelope in dark blue
ink, the stamps set precisely into the corners. She would
have opened them if she hadn't heard the front door creak
and Michael's quick steps mounting the stairs, and she wondered about them for a long time afterward.

Unlike every other boy Gina knew, Michael was a source of
constant frustration. His desire for secrecy she understood,
and even enjoyed sometimes—it was satisfying to sit at dinner with her father, eating her peas and listening to him

gloat about how he had just taken some sucker from Fort Worth in a contract negotiation, with the back of her neck still tingling from where Michael had been kissing it not half an hour before. But it was less satisfying when dinner was over and she was alone in her bedroom, left to reflect that she had never managed to get much beyond kissing, that Michael always disentangled himself just when she thought she had finally seduced him. How it was possible that she had conjured a man all the way to Montana and couldn't get him to go the extra few steps into her bedroom was beyond her.

"How did you grow up to be so pretty in a town like this?" he asked her one night as they sat whispering on a tree stump at the end of her driveway, twilight fading quickly around them, Gina tucking her hair back behind her ears.

"That's brilliant, how many girls have you tried that one on?" she said.

"I mean it. This place is going to turn me into dust," he said. He hooked one finger around the heavy jeweled cross that hung nestled between her breasts, a Christmas gift from her father. "What you need is a place to wear those diamonds," he said. "Keep on living here and they might as well be glass."

"He won't let me leave any more than he will you."

"You don't need his permission. You're an adult. You know what I think?" he said, bringing his mouth to her ear so that his hot breath feathered against her eardrum while he spoke. "I think that deep down, you like being Daddy's girl. Having nice clothes and everyone in town under your thumb. I don't think you really *want* to leave."

Gina turned her head quickly, so that her lips slid against his and she was kissing him hard for a moment before he stood up and stepped away.

"I just can't," he said, "not here. You know he'd find out."

"You're a tease," she said, pulling her knees up against her chest and wrapping her arms around them, turning away from him to look across the fields on the other side of the road. "Anyway, what if he did. I'm old enough to make my own mistakes."

"It's a little different for you. You're his daughter, not some guy he'd beat senseless without a second thought."

"How much do you owe him, anyway?"

"What does it matter?"

"How much?"

Michael was quiet for a long time. Then he said, "Fifty thousand dollars."

"Stupid. Who bets that much money?" He didn't reply, but she could feel the anger in his silence, and looked up at him. "How long 'til you work it off?"

"It's the interest that's the problem. Years."

"Years," she said. "I hope you don't think I'm going to wait that long."

Gina's daddy was sharp, and she didn't kid herself about it. As much as she enjoyed sneaking around, she knew that she was never more than one step ahead of him, that if she wanted to lie, the lie had to be perfect, her face and voice and every detail of her story had to be perfect. But she also had a few trumps on him that he didn't know about, and one of them was the Bomb Drop Money—two hundred grand in cash hidden in the fallout shelter below the basement, Saran-wrapped and ziplocked and stashed in a black gym bag behind four cases of Campbell's Cream of Mushroom soup, right next to the gun rack. She and Laura had found it on a rainy Saturday during Laura's senior year of high school, less than a year before Laura got married and left Gina to fend for herself. They had joked that only their daddy would save money for a day when money couldn't possibly be worth anything, when everyone they knew would probably be dead and they'd be lucky if there was anything left to shoot with the guns, much less buy with the cash.

Now, standing in the cool interior of the shelter with a flash-light gripped in her armpit, Gina counted out stacks of twenties—fifty grand for Michael and twenty thousand more to live on, she wasn't going to be greedy—and then ran her thumb along the edge of the bills, listening to the soft riffle of the paper, like a whispered promise.

She brought the money to the convenience store in her book bag, shifty with anticipation as she waited for Michael to arrive, but when he pushed through the glass door a cool smugness settled over her. She watched patiently as he moved through the store, waiting for the other two customers to leave. When he approached the counter, she scanned the bottle of Coke he handed her and said, "We're running a special today. Buy a pop and get fifty thousand dollars."

"Ha ha," Michael said.

Gina grinned and raised her eyebrows, and nodded to the open book bag behind the counter. Michael leaned toward her and looked down at the bound stacks of bills that she had left at the top of the bag. He coughed once, hard, and stood back again.

"Are you nuts? Where did you get that?"

"Does it matter?" she said.

"Yes, it does matter. If I wanted to get thrown in jail, I could do that on my own."

"It's his, but he won't know about it anytime soon. Anyway, you didn't take it, I did. I could give it to you. Like a gift." She crossed her arms and leaned on the counter, so that the front of her tank top gaped open.

Michael frowned. "What do you want?" he said.

"Take me with you. And we have to go tonight. He'll be at the bar playing poker until close, and then he'll come home drunk and go straight to sleep." She nudged the bag around the side of the counter with her foot. "I could close this place down right now and meet you at the movie theater in an hour. Unless maybe you don't really *want* to go."

"You're loving this, aren't you?" said Michael, but he knelt down and quickly zipped the bag, slung it over one shoulder, and left the store.

...

Gina went home, slipped into a black dress, and packed a bag with some other clothes, a toothbrush and a hairbrush, and an old silver cigarette lighter that her sisters had claimed belonged to their long-dead mother. No nightclothes but lots of underwear and a pair of high heels. She locked the door to her bedroom and turned the radio on, climbed out the window and pulled it shut behind her, already picturing the scene that would take place the next morning. Her father yelling for her to turn down the goddamn music, to haul her lazy butt out of bed and get started on breakfast. Banging on the door and finally breaking it down to find nothing but the radio and a neatly made bed.

She sat on a bench outside the movie theater with her eyes closed, her bag in her lap, the shifting green-yellow-red of the stoplight bleeding through her eyelids as she listened to the street. Michael eased his car up to the curb and called to her softly, and she jumped up and ran around to the passenger side, slinging her bag in ahead of her.

He barely talked while they drove, and when he did his voice was low, as though he were afraid her father could still hear him. They kept on through the night, crossed the border into South Dakota a few hours before dawn. Gina rolled down the window and stuck her head out into the breeze and let out a whoop of excitement, because she had done it, finally, gone farther than her father's influence could reach. A few miles down the road they came to a motel, a cluster of tiny A-frame cabins grouped around a chapel with a green neon cross, and stopped to get a room.

Gina clicked on the bedside lamp and walked around the room opening the drawers, hoping to find something interesting, but Michael sat hunched on the bed and didn't even look at her.

"He's going to find us," he said.

"Hush," Gina said. "No one knows where you are, except me."

"Why did you do it?"

"He has enough to spare some. Did he even ask you where you got it?"

Michael nodded. "I told him I went down to the reservation for the weekend, won it at roulette."

"What did he say?"

"'Some people never learn.' And then he laughed and told me to come back anytime."

She stood in front of Michael, put her hands on either side of his face and tilted it up toward hers. "Stop worrying about him," she said, and then she pulled down her shoulder straps and let her dress slip to the floor like a puddle of ink, just like she'd been studying to do. He drew her to him and pressed his face to her bare, hot stomach. "Oh, Jesus," he said, and he said it all night, but she could tell it was fear the whole time and not her; she had never realized that he was as scared of her father as he pretended to be.

In the next town they came to, they sold Michael's car and bought a used pickup truck with a bed cover, put a mattress in the back and began working their way east as summer started to blaze. In cul-de-sacs and hotel parking lots and gravel pull-offs beside fields of soybeans like rippling green oceans, they made love and fell asleep twined together, the tailgate open to let the breeze play across their skin.

They avoided the interstate and stuck to county routes and two-lane state highways. They sold their phones at the first mall they got to, and Michael used the money to buy a cheap one that they quickly filled with pictures of Gina posing at roadside monuments—giant frying pans and concrete chickens and rhinestone-studded plaster Virgin Marys. Gina called her sisters a couple of times, but the conversations were always so awkward—June sounding confused, Laura angry and jealous, all three of them avoiding mentioning their father—that she gave it up and just sent a postcard now and then. Living out of the truck was uncomfortable, but it was fun in its own way. Sometimes Gina and Michael bathed in truck-stop showers, but more often they filled up buckets in gas-station bathrooms and made do with an empty stretch of country road, him tipping the water over her head while she shrieked and stamped with the cold, throwing her stippled arms around his waist and pulling him to her.

They were too afraid to put anything on a credit card— who was to say her father couldn't use it to track them down—so they just kept spending the cash, but slowly enough that they could pretend it would last forever. In the cities they passed through from time to time, Michael looked up old friends. Gina sat beside him on their couches, smiled when she was introduced, and tried to keep up with the conversation, which was mostly about people she had never met. She drank cocktails when they were offered and tried to be friendly, but she always felt like she made Michael's friends uncomfortable. Even when they smiled at her, she sensed there was something they weren't saying, something on the tip of everyone's tongue, whispered conversations behind closed doors at night. More than once she saw them pull Michael aside, into a hallway or empty room, to talk to him. But those conversations always ended with Michael's laughter as he came back to sit beside her on the couch, where she'd been making painful small talk. The two of them would sleep in the friends' spare rooms or on the sofa, enjoying the hot water and free food and a bed that bounced underneath them. "I don't know how they all got so old," Michael would say, tracing a finger along her spine as she sank into drowsiness. "Must be something about the mortgages." After a few days, he and Gina would say their farewells and move on again, back out on their own, leaving the doubts and hushed voices behind for the old friends to worry about.

They spent the winter traveling the South, as far west as Texas and then slowly back toward Florida.

"Let's head straight up to North Carolina," Michael said one night as they lay together, waiting to fall asleep.

"But I want to see Miami."

"No, you don't. It's just a big overpriced beach full of tourists."

"So what? I like the beach."

"Fine," he said, and turned his back to her, so that she wondered how he could breathe with his face pressed so close against the wall of the truck bed.

They crossed into Florida the next morning, and were still hours away from Miami when Michael turned sharply onto an exit, crossing three lanes to slide onto the ramp at the last second.

"Are we getting lunch?" Gina asked.

"There's something I want to see."

"What?" she said, but he didn't answer, and it was easier to doze with her head against the window than to ask him questions. He never answered questions if he didn't feel like it anyway, and she had become used to his moods.

In the late afternoon they passed through a city and Michael began driving slowly, making turns that took them onto smaller and smaller streets, and eventually onto a dirt road that snaked along for miles.

"Are we near Disney World?" she said.

"Disney World is three hours away. And I'm trying to concentrate."

At last they came to a bend in the road that looked no different from the last dozen curves, and Michael pulled the car onto the berm, just to the edge of the turn, and put it in park, then sat looking out the window, saying nothing. To their left was a house painted bright yellow like a new pencil, with a neatly trimmed lawn bordered by azalea bushes and a red-and-white swing set next to the driveway. An old couple were reclining on lawn chairs next to the swings, the man with a newspaper folded over his face.

"What are we looking at? Are we going to kill these people and steal their car or something?" Gina asked.

"Have you ever been serious for one fucking moment in your life?" Michael said. He leaned forward to see better through the windshield glare.

Gina scowled and turned to look out her window. On her side there was nothing but a dense tangle of plants at the roadside.

"Damn it," said Michael.

Gina looked back at the house. A young woman with a child balanced on her hip had come out to join the older couple. Michael pressed his forehead against the steering wheel.

"Who is that?" Gina said.

"My ex."

"Ex-*wife*?"

"Girlfriend. And my son."

"Huh."

"My life didn't start in your father's mine, you know."

"I'm not stupid," Gina said, but she felt nauseated. The woman had set the little boy down and he was walking across the lawn, grabbing onto pieces of furniture. "Can we go?"

"We will. Soon. I just want to say hello. I want to see him."

"I'm not going in there."

"Good," he said. "Don't. Just wait in the truck, I won't be long."

Gina twisted the edge of her dress around her finger, tight enough to cut off the circulation. "Don't pick him up," she said. "If you pick that little boy up you'll never come back."

Michael narrowed his eyes at her, a cutting look she knew well by now. "Please, be as crazy as possible. Because it's not like this is already hard."

He drove a few miles from the house, taking so many turns and shortcuts that, for a while, she thought he was just driving in circles. Eventually, he parked the car in a gravel lot behind a grocery store.

"Here," Michael said, handing her the cash from his wallet. "Get something to eat while you're waiting. Sorry there's nothing better around."

"I'm giving you three hours, and if you're not back, it's over," Gina said. "I mean it. Don't say you love me, either."

"It won't even be three hours." He grabbed his jacket and got out of the truck.

"I'm going to stay right here and watch for you," she said, but he didn't seem to hear her, walking quickly to the road and starting back the way they had come, sticking his thumb out for a ride whenever a car passed. She watched him until he was out of sight.

She waited there for two days. She ate tuna sandwiches from the grocery store, drank plastic jugs of iced tea, and moved the truck around the parking lot, following the shade of the building as it slowly sailed across the gravel with the passing hours. When she couldn't bear the heat, she'd walk up and down the aisles of the grocery store, pretending to look at canned fruit and boxes of cereal until her blood cooled. As evening settled, she sat with her forehead against the steering wheel and was just starting to doze when some- one said, "Are you all right?"

She opened her eyes. An old man was standing beside the window, looking at her with eyes like puddles of mud.

"Are you all right?" he asked again.

"Fine."

"I seen you out here earlier."

"Who are you?" she said.

"My name's Paul."

"I mean, is this your store?"

"No."

"Then go away."

When she woke up again it was dark, the night full of small noises and the quick sting of mosquitoes, but it was still too hot to roll the windows up. Gina got out of the truck and walked to the edge of the parking lot, looked down to the bend in the road where Michael had disappeared, tried to visualize the yellow house where they had seen the family and the little boy. She imagined Michael sitting there, drinking a beer in the living room, making small talk. She closed her eyes and willed him to stand up, to put the beer down and walk out the door and back up the road to the grocery store and beg her forgiveness. A car came around the bend then, the headlights making her squint, but it roared right past her, spitting gravel at her bare legs. She went back to the truck and climbed inside.

The next day her head ached whenever she moved, and it was hard to even find the energy to get up and go into the store. The thought of drinking more iced tea made her want to gag, but she bought a bag of ice and sat in a patch of grass at the edge of the parking lot, rubbing the cubes across her wrists and legs as the day wore away. At some point, she fell asleep and when she woke up again, it was the middle of the night and the old man was crouching a few feet away from her.

"What are you doing out here?" he said.

"I made him," she said. "He's mine. He has to come back."

"Honey, you're not even making sense. You're tired out. Why don't you come home with me? Whoever you're looking for, you can find him tomorrow."

"He's not, though, is he?" she asked. "Coming back."

Paul helped her to her feet and led her back through the parking lot, empty except for the pickup and another car with the engine running. He walked to the car and leaned in the driver's-side window, said a few words to the man inside, and stood back to let him drive away. Then he came back to Gina and opened the door to the truck, but she made no move to get in.

"I have a granddaughter your age in Boston," he said. "I

wouldn't hurt you for anything. There's a couch in my attic room. You can sleep there tonight, lock the door if you want. In the morning, we can see about getting you home."

"I'm not going home," Gina said.

Paul's house was dark when they arrived. He went around turning on lights, then brought Gina a towel and a washcloth and showed her the bathroom. She didn't bother with a shower, but as tired as she was, she cranked up the air conditioning and lay awake for a long time in the dry cool of the attic, staring up at the peak of the roof and feeling the seams of the couch against her back, trying to think of everything Michael had ever said to her about Florida and love and how beautiful she was.

She woke early the next morning, showered, went into the kitchen and started going through the cupboards. With the radio on low, she began to make pancakes. Paul wandered in soon after, trying to smooth his hair into place with his fingers.

"Smells good," he said.

She nodded, fixed two plates and sat down at the table. Paul ate quickly, swallowing without chewing, like a dog. Gina twirled her fork and leaned back in her chair to look out the window. They didn't speak, until Paul finished his last mouthful and said, "Got some relatives I can take you to?"

Gina thought of June and Laura with their husbands and babies and their boring lives. Of her daddy bubbling with anger, sitting in his bright white office while the miners shuffled through to collect their paychecks. He must know by now that the money was gone, and where to. He might forgive her, but, then again, he might not.

"Not really," she said.

She scratched her fingernail against a spot of crusted food on the tabletop, looked around at the house. The windows were fogged with dust, the kitchen linoleum sticky and curled at the edges. She could smell banana peels in the garbage can under the sink.

"You want a housekeeper?" she said.

Paul set his fork down and sighed. "If I could afford a housekeeper, I'd have one already."

"You need that attic room for anything?" she asked. "You can afford me."

Every morning she served him breakfast, and while he ate she made up plates for his lunch and dinner and put them in the refrigerator, tinfoil pressed down tightly around the edges. Once a week, she went to the grocery store, vacuumed, wiped down the furniture and the windows, and did two loads of wash.

It didn't take long for the attic to wear out its appeal, but she wasn't ready to move on. She took to exploring, learning the layout of the city, walking the sidewalks just to lose herself in a crowd. After a few weeks, she got a job with a catering company and spent her evenings wearing a tuxedo shirt and snug black pants, cruising bar mitzvahs and fundraiser dinners with a silver tray balanced lightly between her hands. On the weekends she and a few of the girls from work would gather at someone's apartment and drink until the early hours, or one of the boys would get up the guts to ask her out, and when she got home in the morning there was no one to answer to, only Paul. He might shake his head as she dragged herself around the kitchen with a blinding hangover, but he never asked questions.

She took her earnings, rolled them up tight in a pillow-case, and hid them in the dark recesses of the couch cush-ions. Some nights she counted the money, smoothing each bill across her knee as she went, a tiny black-and-white TV playing old westerns in the background to keep her com-pany.

One day at breakfast Paul said, "So who was he, anyway?"

"Who?"

"Guy you were waiting on when I met you."

"No one," she said. "Anyway, he ran off with some slut who probably doesn't even appreciate him."

Paul took another bite of his toast. "You ever meet this slut?"

"No. What difference does that make?"

"Just sounds like an ugly name to call someone who wanted the same thing you did."

"Well, I wanted it more," Gina said.

"Did you? Well, it's a hard time getting anything in this life without taking it from someone else."

Gina didn't answer, and Paul went to the counter, poured a second cup of coffee, and set it down in front of her. She blew across the top of it to watch the steam billow off, even though she didn't like coffee.

"When I was your age the only thing I really wanted was a motorcycle," he said. "Never got one. I had a pretty little girlfriend who thought I was Heaven and Earth all wrapped up in Christmas paper, but if someone had offered to let me trade her for a motorcycle, I'd of done it."

Gina laughed. "That's fucked up, Paul."

"Yeah, well. Last I heard, she was living in Naples with her sons and her grandkids, and all I got is a daughter who won't talk to me and a crazy teenage runaway who sulks around the attic all day. And still no motorcycle. So I guess the joke's on me."

She stayed through the summer, months that were hot and steaming and full of the threat of hurricanes, through the fall and the winter, and it felt like time never passed. To her, winter was cold that froze your spit on the pavement, drifts of snow that covered the windows and made the world silent. Here, there was just a slight coolness and some occasional rain. The only thing that told time was the money accumulating like dead leaves, two pillowcases full now, hidden in an old bookshelf behind some coffee cans full of screws. She didn't earn much, but she hardly spent anything. She ate the leftovers from work, prime rib and Coronation Chicken, finger sandwiches for breakfast and slabs of chocolate cake if she had a craving. Sometimes she thought about Michael, wondered if he was even in Florida anymore or if he had gotten himself a new truck and a new girl or just started hitching. She didn't even know the name of the town where he had left her at the grocery store. She knew if she asked Paul he would tell her, and she could drive out there, find her way back to the yellow house, see for herself. She could go crying back to her father, too, say she'd been tricked and taken advantage of, and maybe he'd find Michael for her. But she also knew that the part of her that didn't want to ask for those things was the better part, and so she cleaned the bathroom with bleach water and mowed the lawn and pulled comforters out of boxes to pad the couch and waited without knowing what for.

In May, the weddings started, two or three every weekend. Gina served hors d'oeuvres in ballrooms filled with bunting and candles, extravagant displays of flowers, small pink boxes of candied almonds. She liked the fuss of it all, the ceremony and music and grandparents slow-dancing on parquet floors. She could get overtime when she wanted it, and she always wanted it. One Saturday, Joel, her manager, called to see if she would come down to the Sea Crest to fill in for a girl who was sick.

"What time?" she said.

"Six. But maybe you have a date."

"Not tonight."

"Maybe you should."

She ignored him. Joel was twice her age and said things like this all the time; she expected it as much as he expected her continued rejection.

The room at the Sea Crest was festooned with ugly violet crepe, and the tables were packed close together. As she waited for the guests to arrive, Gina placed napkins beside plates, set out flatware and glasses and silver pitchers of ice water. Joel handed her a basket of favors, chocolate kisses wrapped in tulle with a paper tag attached. *Cheap*, she thought, and set four tables full of them before she saw Michael's name on the tag, paired with one she didn't recognize, his bride's.

Gina turned the tag over and stared at the blank back of it. Flipping it again, she traced her finger over the names, the date. Eleven months since she had come to Florida, and all that time he had been there. Had maybe been at the movies with this woman a few streets away from where Gina was buying shoes, had been happily playing house without ever knowing where Gina had gone or what had happened to her. The thought turned her stomach like a swallow of spoiled milk. She tore the tag free of the chocolates and put it in her pocket, and wove her way through the ballroom to the head table. A chair with a brown plastic booster seat sat beside the bride's chair. Gina filled the water glasses.

Back in the kitchen, she said to Joel, "It's a big wedding, isn't it?"

He shrugged. "About average, really."

"Do you think they love each other?"

"Jesus, are we here to philosophize or are we here to serve shrimp? If we could make money catering divorces the way we do catering weddings, we'd be all over it."

"I'll bet," she said.

Once the guests arrived, Gina kept herself busy refilling platters of cheese and crackers and tried not to watch the door. Finally, the DJ tapped his microphone and announced the newlyweds. The bride and groom entered through an archway decorated with tissue-paper roses, heralded by a song that Michael had always turned off when it came on the radio.

The first thing Gina noticed was how clean Michael looked. In all the time she had known him, he had been smudged with either coal dust or road dust, but now his hair lay flat and his skin looked polished. He smiled and waved at the guests, one arm circled around the waist of his bride.

She was beautiful in an easily forgettable way, soft and smiling and mild as milk. Behind her, being shepherded by an older woman in a pastel suit whose face Gina vaguely recalled from that last day with Michael, was a child of such uncommon loveliness that Gina smiled in spite of herself. He had Michael's curls and his mother's pale skin, and he skipped among his relatives, grasping the hands of the adults as he moved from person to person. Gina clapped with everyone else as the bride and groom took their seats at the head table, watched as Michael leaned over and kissed his wife before settling his napkin on his lap.

Gina bided her time until after dinner. She didn't want to make a scene, exactly; it would be enough to get the bride alone. She waited until Michael had gone off to get a drink and the bride was standing and talking with a small group of people, and then picked up a tray and walked up to her.

"I'm sorry to interrupt," Gina said, "but I wondered if you need a drink? Some champagne or lemonade or something? It's your big day, after all, and we want to make sure you have anything you might want."

"Oh," said the bride. "Some water would be great, actually."

"Of course. I'll be right back."

The water was in sweating silver pitchers on a side table, and as Gina filled a goblet, she watched the bride. Michael's wife was beautiful, but she was nervous. She laughed too much at everyone's jokes, her eyes darting from face to face, and now and then she glanced around the room as if she were lost. Gina placed the goblet on her tray. Moving through the throngs of people who had all gathered to celebrate Michael's marriage, she felt a sense of exhilaration, of power, as though she were a cyclone descending, unsuspected, on all those glad faces. By the time she reached the bride, she could see Michael approaching from the other side of the room.

The bride smiled and reached for the glass, and as her fingers brushed against it, Gina tipped the tray just enough so that the goblet fell forward, sluicing water down onto the bride's dress and soaking it.

A chorus of concerned coos went up from the women surrounding the bride, and people at the nearby tables turned to look.

"Oh, I am so *sorry*, I'm just the clumsiest thing," Gina said. The bride whimpered and began to brush at her skirt, and a woman in a black-beaded cocktail dress said, "Aww," and emptied her drink. Michael was walking quickly toward them now, looking faintly worried, and Gina watched him and waited, and waited, until that moment when he was finally close enough to recognize her. His face turned gray and he stopped in midstride. A man from a nearby table got up and began clapping Michael on the shoulder and congratulating him, and Gina took the bride by the hand.

"Let's go to the ladies' room. I'll fix you right up," she said.

When they reached the powder room, Gina pointed to a chair in the corner and grabbed a stack of paper towels. The woman in the black dress had trailed behind them, and now she leaned against the counter as the bride sank into the chair and Gina knelt down and began to dab at the damp skirt.

"Oh, wow," the woman said, "the dress. Well, I mean. I mean, it doesn't really matter, it's not like you'll have to wear it again. We hope!"

The bride nodded but didn't reply, and Gina turned to the woman and said, "Why don't you go see if you can find a hair dryer to help out here? Try housekeeping."

"OK," said the woman, and staggered out.

As soon as she was gone, the bride made a choking noise and began to cry. Gina dropped the towels and sat back on her heels, bewildered. The bride covered her face with her hands and tried to catch her breath, her shoulders making little shrugging motions that shook the curls pinned to the top of her head.

"I know what everyone's saying," she said. "I know no one thinks it's going to last. But I just wanted him to come home for so long and he did. That must mean something, right?"

Gina looked around, but there was no one else in the room. *Michael's a liar,* she wanted to say. *Michael's a child.* His name itched against her tongue. Every time the bride sobbed, Gina felt her pulse race and her blood sizzle. For the first time in her life, she understood the smile she had seen so often on her father's face, the smile he flashed when he told her about buying out a competitor or twisting the city council around his finger, the one he had surely worn the night he took all of Michael's money. It was a smile that said, *Make the world you want, and take without mercy.* Gina had all the right words; she could make Michael's pretty new life come undone with a wave of her hand.

But she didn't want to. She didn't want any of it— Michael, or the yellow house, or the sweet little boy with his curls. Not the way this woman did. Who knew how many nights *she* had lain awake, wishing with all her strength that he would come back to her. Maybe she had her own kind of magic that had drawn him to the lake that night in Montana, to Gina's dress and the bag of money that had unlocked Michael's chains, all the way across the country and right back to her door. A magic that had gotten Gina free of Montana, which was all she had really wanted to begin with.

A moment later the door swung open and the bride's son ran in, followed by Michael, who glanced around uneasily. He looked at his crying wife, and then at Gina, and as she looked back at him it felt like the last two years had never happened. Like they were still back in Montana standing at that lakeside, staring in the darkness, and she'd just discovered the whole world was a top she could spin with a snap of her fingers.

The bride's tears were turning gray as they dissolved her makeup, leaving sooty trails on her cheeks. She sniffed and swiped at her face with her fingers even as she continued to cry. Gina took one of the towels and blotted the bride's face until it was clean. Then she reached up from where she was kneeling on the floor and grasped Michael's hand, and when he tried to yank it loose, Gina held on tighter. "Help a lady up," she said, and pulled herself to her feet.

MANUS

Zoology, Anatomy: The terminal or distal portion of
the forelimb of an animal, especially a vertebrate,
homologous with or analogous to the hand.

   Roman Law: A form of power or authority . . .

—Oxford English Dictionary

Yvette and I were in bed, watching through a gap in the
curtains as my neighbor Lou Spellman stood at his mailbox
and cried. The corner of the box was pressing into his gut,
and he took a handkerchief from his pocket and wiped his
nose.

   "What do you think happened?" I said to Yvette.

   "Draft card. Obviously. What're you, stupid?"

A woman came out of one of the houses across the street and went to stand with Lou. I'd seen her before, always thought she was pretty, but had never gotten around to talking to her. Now she was rubbing Lou's shoulder while he kept right on crying. I turned away from the window.

"If I was stupid, would you be here right now?" I slid my palm across the sheets, over Yvette's stomach and her breasts. She'd recently gotten her own draft card giving her two weeks' notice, and decided to make the most of things while she could. Most people got only a day's notice, but neither of us was complaining about the extra time—we'd spent the past week holding our own personal Olympics of Sex. Before that, I hadn't seen her in a good ten years.

"I'd still be here if you were stupid *and* ugly," she said. "Don't think you're the first person I called."

I stopped touching her and got out of bed. Yvette was meaner than I remembered. She'd been an art student back when we dated, the only black girlfriend I'd ever had. In her second year of grad school, she'd developed a raging social conscience that meant her apartment was always filled with anti-sweatshop protestors and militant vegans, but before that Yvette and I had spent most of a year holed up in her studio, surrounded by canvases covered in angry swirls of color, getting high and eating junk food and laughing ourselves dizzy. In those days, her body was always flecked with paint, conté crayon caked under her fingernails. At the time I'd told myself it was just meaningless fun, but it looked like a kind of paradise now.

"Hey," she said, coming up behind me and wrapping her arms around my waist. "Don't be so sensitive."

"I have to get ready for work," I said.

The architecture firm I worked for had gotten the contract to design the supplementary housing for the Masters' new American headquarters in Washington, which meant extra hours at the office. A lot of plans were getting scrapped and having to be redrawn, because after seven years we were still learning about the Masters. They despised physical contact, even with one another, so all the hallways had to be three times as wide as we would have made them for people. They hated rough surfaces, so where we would have liked to put carpeting there had to be acrylic tile instead. They didn't need bathrooms. As soon as you thought you'd sorted things out, they would pass down a new mandate: no wood, no windows, as few corners as possible. I was glad we didn't have to figure out the headquarters building itself— another, bigger firm in New York was designing that, although the construction couldn't be started until a third company finished hauling away the remains of the Pentagon.

My co-worker Beatrice called the Masters "the Snots," because that was pretty much what they looked like—giant globs of snot. Every time she said it, I got the same thrill I'd get in elementary school when one of the older kids did something illicit at the back of the bus. Back then I knew I would never be the one to light up a stolen Newport or put my hand up Patricia Riker's skirt, but that didn't cut the vicarious thrill I got from watching other people do it. Beatrice's desk faced the hallway, so I guess there wasn't much chance that any Masters could get in hearing range without her noticing, but I still felt a buzz of adrenaline every time she said, "Oh, goody, another visit from the Snots," or "Guess we'd better add some more troughs to this building so the Snots will have somewhere to eat." She was an older woman, plump, always wearing frilled blouses—she looked like she ought to be at home watching *Family Feud,* which just made her defiance more entertaining. Sometimes when the Masters were standing right by her chair, she'd pluck a tissue from the box on her desk and blow her nose for no reason at all, winking at me from behind her Kleenex.

Bea and I spent most of the morning playing online Scrabble at our desks and sending each other links to hilarious or disgusting Internet videos, but around eleven a Master slithered into the doorway and said, "Hey, anyone who don't have upgrades needs ta go to the conference room." The Masters all had the exact same voice when they spoke English, a high-pitched, androgynous blend of Long Island nasal tones and fat Midwestern vowels. It was indescribably irritating, and no one could figure out why or how they had chosen it as the one über-voice that all of them would use to communicate with Americans. Word was that their versions of Danish and Swahili and every other language were equally grating. I waited until the Master left and rolled my eyes at Bea.

"Have fun, sucker," she said.

"You can't be thinking of words the whole time I'm gone."

"Says who?"

I went into the hall and followed a stream of people down to the conference room. It was a much smaller group than it had been the last time we went through this ridiculous exercise, several months earlier. Once we were all seated, Peggie from HR clicked on the TV, and someone turned out the lights.

The blue screen gave way to the words "Official Re-Handing Procedures," and I probably would have dozed off right then if the video hadn't immediately switched from the title to a close-up of Daniella Cortège. Which I guess was the point. I had seen this same footage at least a hundred times, like everyone else in the world, but I still did a double take when she came on the screen: the flawless face of the Re-Handing Procedures Initiative.

The familiar images continued. Daniella—French, nineteen years old, hot as a cast-iron skillet in a white angora sweater and a tight gray skirt—walks down the hallway of an Exchange Center. She is followed by two Masters, their gelatinous yellow bodies gliding along the floor tiles. Smiling, Daniella walks into the Exchange Room and approaches the blank, buffed zinc face of the "Exchange Apparatus," known to everyone with legs as the Forker. Here was where I always started to think that the Masters were just playing dumb when they said they didn't understand why people complained so much about the re-handing, that, in fact, they had a very good grasp of human aesthetics, because when Daniella holds her hands out to insert them into the Forker, they are ugly: mannish, calloused, the fingernails chewed down to warped little buttons. A blemish on an otherwise breathtaking girl. Without hesitation, she puts her hands into the two dark slots in the face of the Forker, and the pneumatic cuffs hiss shut around her wrists.

Daniella stands for a moment with her hands inside the machine, where they are invisible to the viewer, and to her. She looks relaxed and contemplative, as though she's reflecting on the progress of her life to date, or maybe just on what she should eat for dinner that night. Then the cuffs hiss open again, and she withdraws from the Forker and holds up her arms. Where her hands used to be are five metal fingers, each one fully articulated and as thin as a pencil, connected to a spherical metal base where her palm should be. "Titanium Alloy Hand Upgrades" in Masters' parlance, "forks" to everyone else, because that's what they most resemble. She flexes the tines twice, bends a couple of them at strange angles you could never get with real fingers. Then she opens the little leather purse that's hanging at her side, extracts a compact and a tube of lipstick, and deftly applies her makeup. She nods cordially at the two Masters and walks back down the hall.

Next, a Master comes on the screen and starts describing the draft process, "randomly selected" blah blah blah "everyone will get a card" blah blah. They would go on to say that about ten times before the end of the video, "Everyone will get a card soonah or latah," but by then I was zoned out, wondering what Yvette was up to and whether I was going to get laid this consistently ever again. When everyone around me stood up, I did, too, and went back to my desk.

"Pugnacious," Bea said, looking smug as all hell and cocking her thumb and pointer tines at the Scrabble board like a gun. "One hundred thirty-one points. I guess your little 'pug' was worth something after all."

When I got home Yvette was already there, chopping vegetables in the kitchen, which was full of delicious steam. I wondered whether she'd ever left that morning, but didn't ask. She handed me a broccoli floret. "Feel that," she said.

I pinched the crown of the floret. "Feels like broccoli," I said, and popped it into my mouth.

"No, seriously." She handed me another one. "It's soft, but you can feel all the little buds, too, right? Like taste buds, or goosebumps or something."

"Goosebumps made of broccoli," I said. I ate that one, too.

"You're hopeless." She picked up the cutting board and dumped the vegetables into a frying pan, but when I leaned in to kiss her she set the board down and put her hands on my face, running her fingers through my hair and down the back of my neck. "I always did like your hair," she said. "I knew there was some reason I kept you around."

. . .

That night I woke up to a tapping sound echoing through my bedroom. A moment later, I realized it was coming from the window. I wrapped the sheet around my waist, crossed the room, and pulled the curtains back. Lou was pressing his face against the window, rapping the glass with his fingernails.

"What?" I said. Yvette had gone home earlier, saying she needed a night in her own place, and I was having trouble pulling myself out of the depths of sleep.

"I can't hear you," Lou said, loud as anything, and I pulled the curtains shut, put a robe on, and went around to the back door to let him in.

"What the hell, Lou," I said.

"Listen, I want to talk to you about something."

I sat down in my TV chair and waved him toward the couch.

"Got any beer?" he said.

"In the fridge."

He brought two bottles from the kitchen, handed me one, and sat down again. After he twisted the cap off his beer he just sat there, looking at the dents the cap had made in the meat of his palm.

"So, what's up?" I said.

"I got my draft card today."

"Really? I'm sorry to hear that."

He shook his head. "Me too. I mean, I'm sorry I didn't think about it more before it happened. I guess I wanted to believe I might get lucky. And now it's too late to do anything about it."

"What could you have done anyway?"

"I coulda gone to one of those places. Those surgeries."

"That's an urban legend. Those places don't even exist."

"They exist," he said. "I don't know where yet, but I could find out. I been thinking about it all night."

"Well, I kinda doubt you're going to figure it out between now and tomorrow morning."

"Not for me," he said. "For you. I could find a surgery and if you wanted to do it, I could be your host."

"My what? No," I said. "What would be the point? Nobody likes this, Lou, but you have to man up."

I could see that he wanted to get angry, but he held himself back. "You just think about it," he said.

We drank the rest of our beers in silence, and then Lou let himself out.

I knew I wouldn't be able to sleep, so I clicked on the TV. The only thing that wasn't an infomercial or an old game show was a documentary about President Bolagno, who, as far as I was concerned, had been a total asshole. Everyone would have remembered him that way, too, if he hadn't died in office; being the final U.S. president had done wonders for his approval ratings.

As much as I hated him, I couldn't stop watching once they started the footage of the first official meeting with the Masters. My thumb twitched against the channel button a few times, but didn't quite exert enough force to accomplish anything before morbid fascination won out. It was all completely familiar—the flags flapping, the confetti, Kinshasa O'Brian belting out the national anthem—but I couldn't help getting a little choked up. When Bolagno stepped onto the dais and approached the Master who'd been sent to meet him, when the Master formed a little portion of its glutinous body into an appendage and Bolagno reached out to shake it, I started talking to the TV. It was like watching a horror movie that way, or a rerun of an old football game— I was saying, "No, *no,*" to someone who couldn't hear me, who'd been dead for years and wouldn't have listened to me even if I had been there. Bolagno let go of the Master's appendage, and I knew that already fungus from the Master's body was working its way into his bloodstream, reproducing at an insane rate, that in five minutes I'd be able to see the first black tinge in his skin, and fifteen minutes after that he'd be dead. And yet there he was, smiling like a rock star, hogging up as much time as he could while the All-Father of China and the German chancellor and the Indian prime minister all stood there looking pissed, waiting for their turn to die. I hadn't had any particular love for any of them, either, but I wanted to thank them for throwing themselves on that grenade; it gave the rest of us fair warning.

Eventually the documentary moved on to Bolagno's childhood, and at some point after that I fell asleep, because the next thing I knew it was morning and I was waking up with a stale mouth and a sore back. Half an hour later, I watched through the window as an Exchange Center van pulled into Lou's driveway. Two Masters got out of the van and mushed along up his front walk like two huge balls of slimy Play-Doh. One of them rang the doorbell, and then they started whistling back and forth at each other, carrying on a conversation in their own ridiculous language. For a minute I thought Lou'd decided to make a run for it, but a few seconds later he came to the door, dressed in a suit and tie, and got in the back of the van. The Masters whistled some more, and then they got into the van, too, and drove away.

Lou wasn't back yet when I got home from work, and neither was Yvette, but she showed up at eight with a bottle of good Scotch. Within an hour we were doing shots and making out in the dark when Lou's living room suddenly lit up—his bay window faced mine, and was only about twenty feet away. Lou was still wearing his suit, and he sat down on his couch and rested his elbows on his knees and held up what would have been his hands the night before. He touched the tip of each new metal finger to the metal thumb, and I could just imagine the sound: *click, click, click, click,* repeat.

"Oh, Jesus," Yvette said.

I closed the curtains and we started kissing again, but I could tell she was rattled. Eventually she just stood up and went into the bedroom. I carried the dishes to the kitchen, and before I went after her, took one more peek out the window. Lou was still at it.

The next day was chilly but bright, and Beatrice and I ate lunch outside, at the Chinese restaurant across the street from our office, to try to get a little sunshine before we spent another five hours staring at computer screens.

"Hasn't anyone ever taught you how to use chopsticks?" Bea said. "You look like you're spearfishing." She used her tines to twirl one of her chopsticks like a miniature baton.

Bea had been rehanded at the very beginning of the Exchange, about three years ago, and I couldn't remember anymore whether she had always been this snarky or whether it was something the forking did to her. I was trying to think of a good comeback when I heard someone shouting, and we both looked up.

A van was parked across the square and people were jumping out of it, all wearing rubber suits and gas masks. Another van pulled up behind the first. I grabbed Bea's purse and my jacket, and we ran for the door of our building.

We could hear the gunfire start as soon as we got inside, which meant that the rebels had guns, which meant they were probably not very smart. We took the elevator upstairs to our office and went to the window.

"Those scuba suits were a good idea," Bea said. "And the gas masks. Those cover their whole heads. It looks like they have oxygen tanks, too." She was tapping her forks against the glass with a little *tink tink tink* sound.

"Let's just sit down, Bea," I said. "Please."

"I'm just saying, they look pretty good."

There were maybe two hundred resistance fighters now, more than I'd seen gathered in years. In addition to the guns, they had grenades, which would buy them a little time. They were shooting at the buildings, chipping off bits of stone and breaking the first-floor windows with their bullets. Bea looked at her watch.

Masters started to emerge from the buildings facing the square, sliding through doorways by the dozens, moving the way they always did during these occurrences: slowly, apparently bored. One took several bullets as it slithered to the head of the pack, the ammunition disappearing into its mucous body without ever slowing it. One of the masked fighters threw a grenade, which splattered the closest Master and momentarily flattened the rest of them like squashed caterpillars, while the rebels hunkered down. But a few seconds later, the exploded Master collected its mass back into a single ball and started moving again, and so did the others.

The rebels had grouped themselves around some sort of apparatus in the center of the square, and now they took out what looked like cattle prods, long rods crackling with electricity. They plunged them into the Masters' bodies and someone threw a switch, and for a few seconds you could feel the rebels' anticipation, their hope, even from five stories up. Then each Master belched a little cloud of smoke, and they all surged forward again. This time they engulfed the rebels. For about thirty seconds there was a heaving mass of people and Masters, and then slowly the Masters reversed direction and began to depart, being shot at and pelted with bricks the whole time, ignoring it. It was the most successful riot I had ever personally witnessed. Bea looked at her watch again.

"Did they break ten minutes?" I asked.

"Eight and a half."

The rebels were still running after the Masters, hacking at them with machetes and gun butts, but they were crying, too, because they knew what we knew: If the Masters had turned around, it was already over. The Masters had torn or punched or somehow found minuscule holes in all those bodysuits. They had momentarily pressed tendrils of their slimy bulk against the skin of the protestors, enough to let the fungus take hold. And now they would just let the rotting progress, the way it always did, while they returned to the comfort of their offices.

"Come on, Bea," I said.

"No," she said. "When I die I hope someone has the decency to watch."

The Masters disappeared back into the buildings, and the rebels stood in the square, hugging one another and sobbing, looking up at all of us watching in the offices. I went back to my desk, and twenty minutes later Bea turned away from the window and walked back to her own cubicle, bright-eyed and grim. Only then did I notice that a Master had entered the room at some point and pressed itself against a far window, taking in the scene below. "Buncha loons," it said.

The rebels' bodies were blocking the entrance to the garage where I had parked for work, so I caught a bus home. I took a hot shower and put on jeans and a sweatshirt, heated up a tray of meatloaf, and settled onto the couch. I tried not to think about the protestors, but I must have been thinking about something, because I didn't remember until the doorbell rang that Yvette was coming over. When I opened the door she plucked at my sweatshirt with her fingernails, which she'd had manicured since the day before. Now they were long and blue, with little rhinestone stars on them.

"You wear this just for me?" she said. "Wow." I gave her a hug, and she said, "Sorry. I need a drink."

"How about pot instead?"

"I don't really smoke anymore."

"Neither do I, usually. But it'll be like the good old days."

"These are so clearly not the good old days," she said, but she followed me inside and took the baggie of marijuana I handed her, then sat down to pack a bowl while I heated up a second tray of food.

We ate on my couch, passing the pipe back and forth between bites. As I watched her cut her meatloaf into fastidious cubes and then gobble them like a rabid animal, I wondered whether I hadn't been a little more in love with her than I'd ever been willing to admit to myself, back in our younger days. Yvette sparked up the lighter again and stopped to look at it. "Am I even going to be able to do *this*?"

"You will. I've seen lots of people do it."

She took a hit and handed the pipe to me, leaned back against the opposite end of the couch, kicked off her shoes and curled and uncurled her toes. "My feet stink," she said.

I laughed, coughing on the lungful of smoke I'd been trying to hold in.

"*You* stink," she said. "Stop laughing at me," but she started laughing, too. Soon she was leaning against me, her forehead touching mine. She pressed one finger to my lips, pushed it into my mouth and wriggled it there like a worm, around my tongue, across my teeth.

"Wait a minute," I said, and I moved out from under her and went to the window to close the curtains. Lou was sitting across the way in his living room, staring at his TV with an intensity that confirmed my suspicion that he'd been watching us.

I went back to Yvette and kissed her lips and neck, her wrists, her fingers, all those pulse points, all those tens of thousands of nerve endings. She laced her fingers against the back of my neck and kissed me on the mouth.

"Did you know," she said, "that the Romans used to send prostitutes to prisoners who were about to be executed? I always thought it would be a really sad job, to be one of those girls. Do you feel sad?" She started running her fin-

gers along the waistband of my pants, then unzipped my fly
and slipped her hand inside. "Well?"

"What? No, no, of course not. Could you just . . . yes,
thank you, that," I said. "Just watch your nails."

"You should be glad I still have nails. One day the sight
of someone with fingernails is going to be enough to make
you stop dead in the street."

"Mmmhmm," I said. "You're so right about that."

"Of course I'm right," she said.

I woke up in the middle of the night still on the couch,
Yvette's body wedged between my legs with her head
against my chest. I thought she was asleep, but as soon as I
tried to shift a little to get more comfortable, she opened
her eyes and looked at me.

"Help me," she said. "Please. Let me hide here. Don't
make me go home."

"You know they always catch people who try to run.
They'll find you eventually whether you go home or not."

"But please don't make me," she said.

When I met Yvette she'd been cussing out some complete stranger she'd caught dumping his used motor oil into
the sewer system—"poisoning the rest of us," as she'd repeatedly shrieked. The guy was probably twice her size and
was looking pretty pissed off when I stepped in to help her,
only to find out that she didn't need my help. After five minutes of her lecturing him about the importance of public
waterways, the guy mumbled an apology and fled. That

kind of indomitability was what had drawn me to Yvette, and what drove us apart in the end. She could never just let things *be*—she had to control them, fix them, whether that was a casual polluter or the world or me. But now, for a moment, that was gone, and she was all bare sweetness and trust, looking at me as if I was the one who could fix everything.

"Poor honey," I said, and kissed her forehead.

She pressed her cheek tighter against my chest, but a minute later she pulled herself up and got off the couch.

"Did I do something?"

"No," she said. "Nothing." She went to the window seat, pulled open the curtains, and sat looking out. I knew that in the darkness she was invisible even if anyone happened to be watching, but the ease with which she sat there naked still surprised me. I remembered, now, that she had always been like that, effortlessly nude; in art school she'd painted most of her canvases naked, mixing colors on the skin of her forearm or her hand, and once we'd started having sex she stopped closing the door when she used the bathroom. "You don't mind fucking me but you think it's weird to see me pee?" she'd said, when I mentioned it. "Boy, you are twisted."

Now she reached out and flipped the latches that locked the windows, turned the little crank that set them reeling open, leaned out into the cool night air.

"You know all those rumors you hear?" she said. "That they want to replace our hands so they can program the forks to turn against us, or so we can't use weapons, or because hands remind them of something scary from their home planet? That's all bullshit. It's not a conspiracy, it's just something they do to show us they can. And it won't stop with hands."

"What do you think is next, then?"

"Your dick, probably."

I laughed, but she said, "I'm not kidding. If they control reproduction, they control the whole population. Not to mention what it'll do to morale. You know what a hand job goes for on Birmingham Avenue these days?"

"Of course not," I said. "Do *you*?"

"More than sex, I know that much."

"Come back over here. It's getting cold."

She reached her hands out the window and waved them slowly back and forth. "I'm leaving," she said, "just give me a minute."

"I don't want you to leave."

She shrugged, as if to say that what I wanted didn't matter much. I walked over and stood behind her with my hands on her shoulders, and she kissed my thumb and got up to start collecting her clothes.

"Why don't you just spend the day here tomorrow," I said. "I'll call off work. We can go to a movie or something."

She finished dressing and stood in front of me, her high heels clutched in one hand. The top of her head came up only to my chin. She took hold of my hair, not all that gently, and pulled my face toward hers for another kiss. "You're exactly the same as you ever were," she said, when we separated again.

"Thank God for small favors, huh?"

She looked at me very seriously for a moment, but all she said was, "Good night, Aaron." I wrapped myself in a blanket, walked her to her car, and watched her taillights until she turned onto Parkvale and disappeared.

The next day I kept checking my phone, hoping she'd text me and say she wanted to spend the night. Around eight o'clock I gave her a call, but she didn't answer, and she didn't show. I knew she was due at the Exchange Center the following day and wouldn't come to see me after she'd been forked. And I didn't really want her to. More than anyone else I could think of, Yvette would be diminished by the forking, subdued in a way that was antithetical to her nature, and that I didn't want to witness.

The week that followed brought the first really warm days of the year. I got home from work on Wednesday and found Lou in his backyard loading his grill with charcoal. He winced a little every time his metal fingers scraped on the metal of the grill. That was one way you could tell people who had just gotten their forks—that sound still bothered them. From what I heard, you got used to it soon enough. He disappeared inside, and came back a while later with a plate of hamburgers. He made great burgers, with diced onions and garlic mixed right into the meat. They smelled incredible while they were cooking, and I knew all I had in the house was a bag of frozen corn and some ramen; I couldn't help glancing over now and then. When the burgers were half-cooked, Lou flipped a few of them with a spatula. But then he reached out and grabbed one with the tips of his metal fingers and turned it over just like that. He did the rest of them that way, and when they were finished he picked them up and put them on a clean plate, and wiped the grease off his tines with a paper towel. Then he knocked on his window, and a minute later, a woman came out carrying a plate of buns, with a bottle of ketchup pinned under one arm. She looked way too hot to be hanging out with Lou, and I realized that she was the neighbor I had seen consoling him on the day he got his draft card.

She went back into the house for a blanket, and they both settled down on the grass to eat.

"Like a burger?" Lou called to me.

"Sure would." I hauled my chair over to his side of the lawn.

Lou put his fork gently on the woman's shoulder. "This is Mary Ellen. She's our neighbor."

"Yeah," I said. "Hi."

She smiled, a nervous little smile, and handed me a burger. I hunched forward as I bit into it so the juice would drip into the grass. When I straightened up again, Lou and Mary Ellen seemed to be in the middle of a pantomime, which they quickly dropped. Mary Ellen shot Lou a look, and he cleared his throat.

"We're going out on Saturday night," he said. "Maybe you wanna join us?"

"Bowling?"

"No."

"I don't want to be a third wheel, Lou. Thanks anyway."

"It's not really a date," he said.

Mary Ellen leaned forward and put both her hands on my knee. Her fingers were trembling. "It would be nice if you'd come along," she said. She had a quiet soprano voice, as sweet and grainy as a sugar cube.

I knew that if I didn't go, I'd spend the whole weekend at home with nothing to do, meditating on the feel of Yvette's tongue against mine, slightly dry from the pot, remembering the way she had stared at me before she left.

"Sure," I said.

I woke up at six o'clock the next morning to the doorbell ringing incessantly and rushed to answer it, wading through a half-dream of Yvette standing there, hands and all, smiling wryly at me. Instead, I opened the door and found myself standing in my boxers with my belly dangerously close to the viscous surface of two Masters. They both slid back a few inches.

"Howyadooin," the one closest to me said, not as an actual question, just as preamble. They tended to start conversations that way. "We're lookin' for this woman. Ya seen her?"

The other Master extended an appendage that was looped loosely around a small pixel frame showing a head shot of Yvette. It was an old picture, from about the time when I'd first known her. She looked like she was considering biting the cameraman, whoever that had been.

"Yes," I said.

"Where's she at?"

"I don't know. At home, I guess. The last time I saw her was days ago."

"Ya haven't seen this woman since then?"

"No," I said. "No, and I haven't talked to her either."

The Masters whistled back and forth a bit, and the one with the pixel frame said, "This woman is wanted for re-handing evasion. If ya see her, ya must report it immediately."

"Evasion?"

"She has failed to show up for her appointment. This is her last known location. Ya sure she ain't here?"

"No," I said. "I mean, yes, I'm sure."

The Masters talked to each other again, and then the nearer one said, "Seeing as how we're already here, ya might as well come wid us."

"Come with you where?"

"To the centah," said the Master, producing an appendage and extending it toward the car they had both driven up in. "We don't have no more evasion appointments today, so we might as well take you for re-handing."

I stood with my hand on the doorframe and didn't say anything. A cold wash of adrenaline hit me and my brain was ticking so fast I thought I might pass out. I wanted an excuse, any excuse, even if it would buy me only one more day.

"I haven't had a draft card," I said. "It's not my turn yet."

"Nah, it don't matter," said the Master holding the pixel frame, retracting the tendril-like appendage back into itself, so that its body swallowed up Yvette's picture, frame and all. "Everyone will get a card soonah or latah. We can enter it into the computah when we get there. It won't be no problem."

"But I'm supposed to be meeting someone," I said. "I'm going to visit a friend in the hospital. He's very sick. And anyway, I'm not even dressed."

"Yeah," said the Master, moving toward the car. "It won't take that long. We'll tell them to put you first." The other one advanced toward me, closer by inches until I took a step away from the door, toward their car. The Master flattened itself until it was almost a plane and slid behind me, so that I had to either step forward again or touch it, and began shepherding me toward the car.

"I just don't think this is a good idea, doing this out of order," I said.

"Yeah, okay, it'll work out just fine," said the Master behind me, manifesting an appendage and opening the car door for me.

• • •

When I got to work the next day, Bea was sitting at her desk, with her nose practically pressed to her computer screen.

"What're you watching, Bea?"

"Shhh," she hissed at me, and motioned me over without taking her eyes from the monitor. I stood behind her and watched a group of surgeons gather around a shrouded table.

"What is it?" I said.

"*That* is the new revolution, if you ask me," she said. "Pretty wild stuff. And this video has about a billion hits already. It keeps getting taken down and then someone else reposts it, and then people post responses, and it's all over Chatterbox and VolkBytes. There have been riots, even. There's this woman, right, and this team of surgeons is operating on her—"

"Maybe another day, Bea," I said, and she immediately turned around in her swivel chair, looked me up and down, and pulled my arms from behind my back. Beatrice doesn't miss anything.

She stood up and folded me into a hug. "I'm sorry, I really am," she said, at which point I started to cry, something I'd had no inkling of doing before that moment. I had spent the previous night watching TV and trying not to look at my forks, drinking gin from a paper cup because the sound of the tines on a beer bottle irritated me, eating pizza with my eyes closed so I wouldn't have to see them. I had told myself several hundred times that it was normal, that in fact the forks worked fine and it was happening to everyone and it was no big deal, but Beatrice made it impossible to believe any of that. She turned off her computer monitor and grabbed her box of Kleenex, and shuffled me into the supply closet, where, as I leaned my head against a ream of copy paper and cried, she pulled out a stepladder, climbed it, and popped the battery out of the smoke detector. When she climbed back down, she fished a pack of cigarettes out of her pocket and jammed two of them into her mouth, side by side, so she could start them both before handing one to me. I accepted it and took a movie-style drag that left me hacking and gasping for breath.

"Such a Boy Scout," Beatrice said.

I held up one fork with the three middle tines raised. "Thrifty, loyal, clean, kind, and obedient, ma'am."

"Those bastards," she said. "We should soak them all in napalm and toss them a match."

We stayed in the closet until she had finished her cigarette and mine had burned down to the filter, and then she straightened my suit jacket and swung open the door and we went back to our desks and got to work.

The next night my phone rang three times in an hour, and eventually Mary Ellen came over and knocked on my door. When she saw my forks her whole face scrunched up like she was going to cry, but a moment later she got hold of herself and said, "Come on along anyway," and led me over to Lou's house.

"Forked," she said, and Lou looked down at my would-be hands and sighed.

"Let's get going," he said.

We got in Lou's car and he started driving, out past the suburbs, into the exurbs. He turned onto a small street, and then down an alley. On either side of us were huge warehouses, most of which looked like they'd been empty for years.

"What is this?" I said.

"Just wait." We were pulling up in front of a warehouse with a blue light shining from one wall. Two huge doors were open ahead, and when Lou drove through them we were suddenly inside a cavernous, dark room where lanes had been marked out using flares. He found a parking space and led me to a door that took us into another alley, where we entered another huge warehouse.

The second building had been set up like a school cafeteria—row after row of folding lunch tables with people standing on top of them, small spotlights at their feet. All the people standing on the tables were what Lou would have called "hosts"—they had forks like anyone else who'd been "upgraded," but they also had at least one pair of human hands attached somewhere on their bodies. There was one woman with a half-dozen pairs down her back, another with several pairs clustered on her hips like frills. One man was so covered in hands that he looked like a giant coral colonized by anemones, all those fingers waving in a current only he could feel. Some of the hands had the nails carefully shaped and painted, but there were workmen's hands, too, large-knuckled and calloused, with grease and dirt ground into the skin. The whole place had the feel of a third-world street market, vendors crowded together and people wandering through testing the wares, eating snacks from the concession stands that had been set up here and there between tables, haggling, carrying gossip back and forth across the aisles.

Now and then you'd see someone step up onto one of the seats attached to the tables—those orange plastic seats where I had eaten years of tuna sandwiches in my youth—and touch the symbiotic hands, feel the texture of the skin and the strength of the fingers. Sometimes the person touching and the host would go off together toward the back of the building, which Lou told me was where they had set up a surgery for hand transfer.

"An hour and you're done," he said. "Most of the procedure's automated at this point."

"But what do people do without hands?"

"You can go to an Exchange Center the next day and claim that you had them removed yourself because you couldn't stand them anymore. You get forks just like anyone else, and the Masters eat that shit up, like, 'Oh, finally, this one has seen the light.' They don't get what we're doing here."

"I can't say I entirely get it either."

"Think about it. They're like—like endangered animals, or something. We gotta keep them alive somehow. We can't just let those blobs take 'em from us."

"How the hell did you even find this place, Lou?"

He shrugged. "I know some people. Check this out." He pulled me over to a table where a tall redheaded woman stood, wearing nothing but high heels and a black velvet choker. Her skin was so pale you could see her veins, and she had four pairs of hands—a chocolate brown pair blooming between her breasts like dark flowers, and another three pairs in varying shades that wrapped around her calves, all of them men's hands from the look of them. Her forks were so covered in sparkling rings that you could hardly see the metal, but the fingers of all the human hands were bare.

The woman next to her had creamy brown skin and wore a yellow knit dress that hung low on her shoulders; around her collarbone a pair of ivory-white hands were clasped like a necklace. The two women on the table were talking to each other, not even paying attention to us. I knew I was staring, but so was Lou, and neither of us seemed to be able to stop.

"Can I touch them?" said Mary Ellen. She was so quiet it was easy to forget she was there, but now her rusty little voice cut through the din.

The two women stopped talking, and the black woman looked down at her. "First time here?"

"Yes."

"Hold up your arms," the host said, and when Mary Ellen showed her hands the woman said, "All right. I think they like a little touch now and then anyway."

While Lou and I watched, Mary Ellen stepped onto the chair and up to the table. The host touched the hands that were growing around her neck, caressed the white fingers with her tines, so that they separated and stretched. They were delicate hands, the fingers tapered and graceful. I could easily imagine them playing the violin, or shaping clay into pots.

"Aren't they beautiful?" the redheaded woman said. "They're from a woman we used to work with at the Department of Public Health."

"Where is she now?" Lou said.

"Still there, I guess. We haven't been back since we became hosts. Too risky."

The other woman nodded to Mary Ellen. "Go ahead."

Mary Ellen touched one of the pale fingers tentatively with one of her own. Then she pressed her palm against the other hand's palm, and the fingers meshed together and gripped.

"They feel just like real fingers," Mary Ellen said.

"They are real fingers," the redheaded woman said.

Mary Ellen stroked the backs of the symbiotic fingers with her free hand, and the black woman closed her eyes and sighed.

"You have a nice touch. Warm," she said.

I wanted to climb up on the table and join them, but I

knew I couldn't, and I felt the same tightness in my chest that had ambushed me at the office with Bea. When Mary Ellen pulled her hand free, the fingers clung to her, as if they wanted to hold on a little longer. She turned to look at Lou.

"Well?" he said.

Mary Ellen nodded. "Yes."

"You sure?"

"Yes," she said.

The black woman hugged Mary Ellen, and the redhead pulled a ring off one of her tines. "Here you go, girlfriend. For good luck," she said.

Mary Ellen climbed down off the table and took hold of Lou's left fork, and they talked for a moment with their heads close together, glancing toward the back of the warehouse. Lou took his car keys out of his pocket and gave them to me.

"Here," he said. "We won't be able to drive afterward anyway, not for a few hours at least, while the anesthesia wears off."

"Where should I meet you?"

"Go home when you're ready," he said. "Someone'll give us a ride."

I watched them leave, and when I turned around the two women were climbing down from the tables. I noticed several of the other hosts doing the same. From the center of the room, I could hear a swell in the general clamor of the crowd. The women headed toward the noise, and I followed them.

• • •

A long stage had been set up, a proper stage, not just another lunch table, with pink lights and a sound system. People were queuing up at one end of it, and then music came blaring out of the speakers and people began to walk across the stage.

The man next to me explained that they were all the new hosts who had accepted hands since the last meeting. Some strutted like they were born to be on a catwalk, and others were shy. I imagined Lou up there at the next gathering, Mary Ellen's dainty transplanted hands cradling his gut. The audience applauded continuously, a mix of flesh slapping flesh and the tang of metal on metal.

At the very end of the line was a group of people wearing loose blue robes—choir robes, I realized. There were a lot of them, maybe twenty, and as they crowded together at the end of the stage an announcer finally appeared from somewhere to proclaim in a tinny voice, "Ladies and gentlemen, our special guest of the evening."

The music kept playing and the din from people in other parts of the building rumbled on, but everyone around me stopped talking. The people with the choir robes climbed up on stage and disrobed all at once, and immediately I could see what had everyone so intrigued. These people had gone beyond hands; what they were hosting was an entire human being, carved into pieces and distributed among them. The symbiotic body—dark-skinned, female—surfaced and submerged across their bodies like the coils of a sea serpent breaking the skin of the ocean. Here a breast, there a set of toes, here a swell of flesh that could have been a calf or a forearm or the skin that wrapped the ribs. As I watched, they began to form clusters, to display whole sections of the woman they were hosting—a woman whose body, with each passing second, looked increasingly familiar. The hands had gone to a man who was standing near the middle of the stage, and when I looked more closely I saw that they had long, shaped fingernails, painted a color that in the rosy light could have been blue or could just as easily have been green or lavender. One of the fingers curled and I swore I saw the twinkle of a rhinestone. The crowd around me began to stamp their feet and roar.

I turned away from the stage. Standing next to me were two girls who looked about sixteen. One wore a green tube dress that was too tight for her, and she was bouncing on her toes with excitement, screaming and stomping. The other was chewing a piece of her hair, winding another piece around her finger. I wondered when teenage girls would stop winding hair around their fingers. When the Masters would start forking children at birth, so that they'd never even know what it was like to have real hands, so that whole portions of their brains would remain dark and unused.

The girl in the tube dress noticed me looking at her and smiled. "Isn't this just blazing? I can't believe we're here for this," she said.

"I think I know that woman," I said, even though saying it out loud kicked a wave of queasiness into my stomach.

"Which one?"

"That one." I gestured at the lineup of hosts, still refusing to look. "The one that's all of them. I think she's my old girlfriend."

The girl's eyes got big. "No *way*," she said. "Yvette Raymond was your *girlfriend*?"

The nausea settled deeper, but I nodded. "Do you know her?"

"Well, I mean, not personally, but she's the reason we came tonight. I mean, her video is just *incredible*, and when she's like, 'We can't submit, we have to do *something*' and she lets those doctors just start cutting her *up*? I mean, my head pretty much exploded," the girl said. "And she's totally right. We outnumber those nasty slugs by about a thousand to one and we're just *sitting* here?" She pulled her phone out of her purse and started recording the people posing on stage.

"They'll never get her now," the other girl said. "We can't let them get any more of us." She spoke quietly, without her friend's percolating enthusiasm, but I could see in her face the kind of passion that made people lie down in front of tanks and smuggle refugees over borders in car trunks, that made them burn bras and flags and draft cards.

It was a passion I couldn't share, as much as I knew Yvette would have wanted me to. Instead, I felt a completely unrevolutionary longing for the woman these girls would never know, the one who examined vegetables as if life depended on it and mixed blue into green in the palm of her hand. If I turned back to that stage, if her rebellion ignited a mutiny that saved us all and her face covered every billboard on the planet, still, I would never really see her again. No one would, not even the hosts who carried her defiance in a moving mosaic, who pumped the blood through her body and shared the sparks in her nerves.

PLEIADES

Del

My parents were geneticists. They had a firm belief in the power of science to fix everything, to create everything. This belief was their religion, and they liked to proselytize as much as any born-again Christian. When they decided to have children, they saw the opportunity to share their faith in science with the world. They wanted to make miracle babies so unbelievable that people would stop and stare, their own organic equivalent of a billboard for Jesus. Their original idea was to develop an in vitro procedure that would create identical twins. But they decided twins weren't spectacular enough, not enough of a challenge. They settled on septuplets. One fertilized egg split into seven pieces made seven sisters, all of us identical. Pleiades, my father used to call us, after the constellation of seven stars.

All the major networks were shooting footage at the hospital the day we were born. Protestors traveled from around the country to Los Angeles so they could picket outside, with signs that said SEVEN DEADLY SINS and FRANKEN-STEIN'S CHILDREN. Even the doctors who delivered us expected us to come out with birth defects; half a dozen neonatal specialists were standing by. But they weren't needed. We were small—about two pounds each—but other than that, my mother says, we were perfect. Our lungs, our hearts, our brain activity were measured and found to be normal. We all had a wisp of dark hair at the front of our foreheads, and eyes that would turn from blue to brown. My parents didn't want rhyming names or alliterative names, but they liked to show off their knowledge of Greek, and so we were Leda, Io, Zoe, Helen, Cassandra, Vesta, and me, Adelpha, called Del.

In the magazine photographs, my mother and father glow with a mixture of parental pride and professional elation. Without scientific interference, identical twins account for one in every 250 live births, identical triplets one in two million, fraternal septuplets one in every four million, and my sisters and I just couldn't exist. But science made us and there we were, pink-skinned and button-nosed, each swaddled in her own colored blanket—red, orange, yellow, green, blue, indigo, purple—a wriggling, blinking rainbow.

The tabloids ran headlines like "Forced Septuplets Really Alien Babies!" and "Test Tube Septs Share One Brain!" After our first birthday, the publicity died down, although reporters came around now and then hoping to do follow-up stories. In the scientific community, our celebrity never waned. Throughout our childhood we took trips to visit scientists whom our parents referred to as our aunts and uncles. These people smiled at us and sometimes gave us hugs like real relatives, but they also liked to look at our skin cells under microscopes, or watch us play together through two-way mirrors. My mother and father ran experiments, too, and by the time we were six, we thought no more of giving a blood sample than we did of making our beds, picking up our toys, or any other chore.

Our parents never told us which of us was born first because they thought it would affect our psychology. We reached the age of eleven considering ourselves separate in body, but not in anything else. I have heard that twins, even identical twins with a particularly close relationship, like to emphasize that they are still individuals, but we did not. There's an old home video of us on the beach, eight or nine years old and wearing matching gold-spangled swimsuits. We move across the sand like a flock of birds in flight, each head turned only a fraction of a second before the next, so it's impossible to say where one motion ends and another begins.

Perhaps it was the circumstances of our creation. Perhaps we were not truly separate people but parts of a whole, as a thicket of aspen trees all grow from the same network of roots. And, even now, maybe it is no different.

"You were so easy, really," my mother said to me a few years ago in tearful nostalgia. "You all liked peas, you all hated carrots. No one would use the pink crayons."

Who knows what would have happened if we had reached high school together, been forced to deal with romances and social intrigues and the possibility of attending different colleges. Perhaps we would have simply refused to be parted, clung together like a cluster of ladybugs in winter. Or maybe we would have adjusted, moved apart and away from one another. But I doubt it.

We were eleven years old, doing a jigsaw puzzle on the living room floor of our beach house in Santa Cruz. Vesta set a corner piece in its place, put her hand to the side of her head and said she had a headache. We all looked at her and groaned; headaches had a way of catching among us, even though our mother tried to tell us that was impossible. A few minutes later, Vesta shook her head and complained again, and then she fainted, we thought. But we had a horrible clenched feeling in our bodies. Leda put her hands on Vesta's cheeks and Vesta didn't even flinch. We all went screaming for my mother.

At the hospital they said my sister had had a brain aneurysm, that she was dead. We wanted to argue, but we knew it was true. We could feel it. That night we all slept piled on the floor of our bedroom, holding on to one another's wrists and calves and hair, terrified of losing one another. For months after that we felt sick, but we thought it was just sadness. We didn't know yet that for us there was no such thing as *just* sadness, that our grief had a life of its own, an invisible mouth like a black hole that drew us inexorably closer.

We were twelve when Leda got pneumonia. She never recovered. The doctors put her on every antibiotic they had, but she was dead in three weeks. Again my sisters and I felt that same tautness in our bodies, that surge of poison in our veins, but we kept quiet about it. We didn't need to discuss it with one another, and our parents didn't understand anything. They were depressed, guilty, frantic for the solution they felt sure must be out there just beyond their reach, but that didn't touch what we felt. We were all thinking, without ever saying so, that one death might be a freak accident, but two was not. That we were all going to die.

Reporters followed us everywhere. There were Internet betting pools about which of us would die next. We started exercising, eating organic food, taking vitamins as if that was going to help. Another year went by and we lost Io. Antigenetics protestors swarmed her funeral, glowing with self-righteousness. One woman carried a sign that said "Science Giveth and the Lord Taketh Away." She wore a lime-green sundress and stared at us through the wrought-iron fence of the graveyard during the entire service, never making a sound.

The remaining four of us began developing bruises in

places we couldn't remember bumping. We were flown to specialists around the country, circulatory doctors, immunologists, gene therapists; we gave countless samples of blood and urine and tissue, were prodded and analyzed without receiving any conclusive results. They thought we had a new form of AIDS, or had somehow developed hemophilia, but none of the tests supported these theories.

Eventually our parents moved us to New York City so they could set up camp at Mount Sinai Hospital and put all their energy into trying to cure us. They weren't medical doctors and didn't really belong there, but I believe there was a bargain struck, something to do with donating our coveted tissue samples, the kind of utterly calculated deal I didn't want to know too much about. I've always believed that the move had as much to do with getting away from their colleagues in California as it did with saving us; my parents were not so gracious in their defeat as they had been in their glory.

When Zoe got sick, the rest of us began to consider desperate solutions. The three deaths we had suffered through were horribly painful, to be sure, but in a way the most difficult, the most shocking, the most surprising, the worst thing was finding ourselves still alive the next day. We felt mocked, being forced to face, time and again, this brutal proof of our distinctness. We decided to bring it to a neat end, for all of us, if Zoe didn't improve.

By then we were sixteen, old enough to be crafty, to filch chemicals from our parents' lab that were sure to be fatal.

We kept them in little vials in our pockets as we stood around the hospital bed. But at the crucial moment—heart monitor flatlining, alarms sounding, frantic nurses attempting resuscitation—we failed to act. Not one of us so much as moved a hand toward the poison. We still wanted to live in spite of it all.

The next time we didn't consider the plan again. We just sat silently by Cassie's bedside, kissed her tears, and watched her go. Then it was me and Helen, and we were terrified and sick all the time. We kept wondering which one of us would die next, wondering whether it was worse to be dead or alive and alone.

We dreamed about the others. Sitting down to dinner or choosing our clothes for the day, we sometimes hesitated, waiting for them without realizing what we were doing. Their breath filled the room, their fingertips were on our skin. Helen and I began to feel stretched, overfilled, over-sensitive to everything. Loud noises frightened us beyond reason. The sound of our parents yelling or crying, both of which they did frequently, made us dizzy.

Helen started having trouble breathing. We were eighteen and it would have been the year of our high school graduation, but we'd long since quit school. For the next five years, she was battered by a drawn-out illness, waves of health and sickness lifting her up and throwing her down again. My parents whisked in and out of our house like ghosts in their fluttering white lab coats, going back and forth to the hospital to examine cultures under the micro-

scope, visit Helen, or meet with another doctor promising a
cure. By then I could have told them exactly what was
wrong: The emotion and sensation of seven people con-
densed into two bodies was too much for the bodies to bear.
But that was an explanation that wouldn't satisfy the rigors
of science, so I knew it wouldn't satisfy them. There was
nothing they could do about it anyway.

Helen kept saying to me, "What will we do?" Her skin
looked like it had shrunk, tight and shiny across her bones.
There was nothing to say because we both knew the answer:
"We" would not do anything. She would die, and I would
stand in the damp grass of the cemetery with no one to
squeeze my hand at the graveside. My parents were around,
of course, but I'd grown up without having to speak my
mind, and I never knew what to say to them. Besides, I was
finding them increasingly hard to love. I kept thinking about
that protestor at the funeral, years ago now, and an idea
began tormenting me: Maybe there was only meant to be
one of us. Maybe all that splitting had been a bad idea. I
missed my sisters, but it was more than that. I could feel
enough for seven people, as if my sisters wanted me to live
for them. I wondered if Nature, once she had pared us
down to one body, would let me survive, or if it would just
be worse for me in the end.

My parents were desperate. They began planning to
clone me or freeze me if I died, plotting it in their bedroom
at night, never thinking I might be listening from the hallway. Despite their collusion, they hated each other. They

both wanted me to forgive them for whatever mistake in their calculations had brought this on us, to forgive them on behalf of my sisters, too. Surely, I could. Surely, I was all of us in one.

But I couldn't, or maybe I just didn't want to. I felt my sisters in me and around me and I knew that, whatever pain awaited me, letting my parents decide my fate was the worst choice I could make.

"Go," said Helen. "Maybe you can outrun it. If one of us is left, that's enough."

Troy

A car comes down the road, an old blue hatchback covered in dust, and it slows down just when I've decided it's not going to stop.

I'm pretty good at choosing cars by now; I can almost tell by the way they roll down the window whether to trust the driver or not. But when I look inside, it seems to me I judged wrong this time. The girl behind the wheel looks like a zombie, skin falling off her, patches of hair missing. She could be twenty, thirty, I don't know; she's so messed up it's hard to tell.

"Where are you going?" she says.

"L.A."

"I'll be passing near there."

It's something about the way she looks at me, not threatening but not afraid, that makes me get in. Besides, it's not often you find a ride that'll take you through ten states, and I'm in no position to be picky.

Two hours down the road we blow a tire and the spare's no good. We wait for a tow truck, then eat supper at a diner in town while the tire gets patched. I order chicken-fried steak and she eats a fruit salad. She saves all the grapes for last and slides each one over her tongue like a marble. "I can taste the sunshine," she says.

When she opens her wallet to pay the waitress, it's stuffed thick with cash. She plucks off a hundred-dollar bill to pay a twelve-dollar tab, and there's another hundred underneath. It's enough to tempt even an honest man.

"You always carry money like that?" I ask. "It's not safe."

She smiles a little, her lips full of cracks like old rubber ready to split. "Neither is picking up hitchhikers, but that didn't seem to bother you."

"Still."

She waves a hand at her blistered face. "Look at this," she says. "I'm past the point where I worry about something bad happening to me."

We pick up the car but it's late to be starting out, so we get a motel room for the night, two beds, cable TV. She falls asleep right away, and her breathing gets so quiet I worry a couple of times that she's dead, and lean over her bed to check. In the middle of the night, though, she begins to moan. She's still asleep, her eyes roaming back and forth underneath the lids, tears slipping between the lashes. I turn the bedside lamp on but it doesn't wake her, and I'm afraid to touch her now. I sit on my bed with my hands in my pockets, edge of the headboard cutting into the back of my neck, wondering how long the walk is to the next bit of civilization. Wondering whether you can really leave a girl to die alone in a motel room, and what to do if you stay.

She wakes up just after sunrise looking worse than ever, which I wouldn't have thought was possible. She sits on the edge of the bed with her face in her hands.

"I don't know if I can do this by myself," she says.

"Let me drive for a while," I say.

When we get on the road we talk a little, but I can tell she doesn't like conversation much. She starts peeling the dead skin off her arms, piece by piece like she's stripping wallpaper, absentminded the way that some people chew their fingernails.

"Stop that," I say, and she looks up and kind of smiles, sheepish, and folds her hands in her lap. "What's wrong with you, anyhow?"

"I'm sick," she says, like that's all there is to it. "Don't worry, you can't catch it."

"Does it hurt?"

"Usually."

"Don't you have a doctor or something?"

"Dozens of them," she says.

I look her up and down. "Well, I guess they aren't worth a damn, are they?"

We both laugh. She looks different when she laughs, like there's a brightness spreading through her face, like the sound fills her whole self and not just her mouth.

"You should have flown, though. It would've been easier on you."

"It wouldn't," she says. "It makes me vomit these days. Besides, this was a last-minute decision, and now I get to see what's between New York and California."

"What are you aiming to do when you get there?"

"Go to the beach," she says, as if she was just another sand bunny in a string bikini, a bored college girl on spring break with nothing else to do.

We drive and talk about the music on the radio, movies, the weather. She sleeps a lot, her head resting against the window, hands balled together in her lap, a pained look on her face the whole time. I wonder if her body hurts even in her sleep, if she's healthy or ravaged in her dreams.

Partway through Illinois we hit a nasty snarl of traffic. Somebody's dead up ahead, judging by the number of cop cars and ambulances that go screaming past us along the shoulder of the road. We're near an exit, so we escape after a few minutes, get ourselves onto Route 66 and stop for lunch at a roadside burger joint, one of those chains that used to cover the country but now exist in only a few god-forsaken outposts. They have a picnic table to the side, wood gone gray and full of splinters, on a patch of dead scrub grass and hard-packed red clay. We take our food out there. Del licks the salt off her fries but doesn't eat them, just watches me with my hamburger.

"What's the matter?"

"I don't eat meat anymore," she says.

"Maybe that's your problem."

She shakes her head, chews on the end of one fry while she stares at the dirt between her feet.

"You can have these," she says, pushing the paper sleeve of french fries at me. She gets down on the ground and starts scratching at the dirt with her fingernails, and at first I think she's looking for something, but then I see she's just making a pile of red dust. She scrapes some more, picks up a stone to do a better job, working with all her strength.

"What the hell are you doing?"

Instead of answering, she takes her waxed paper cup from the table, dumps half the soda out of it and scoops the dirt in. She sits down again and I watch her stir the whole mess together with her straw until it's like pudding, and then she starts spooning that slop into her mouth.

"Stop it or you're gonna be sick for sure," I say, but she keeps going. I grab her arm and let it go again. Her skin is too hot. Her bones feel like they could crumble in my hand. The more time I spend with her the clearer it is to me that she should die, that dying would be good for her. When she can't eat any more, she wipes her mouth on her sleeve and leans her elbows on the table.

"Sometimes I feel like I'm just going to fly apart. Like nothing in me is solid," she says. "Who's to say what fixes that?"

I throw the rest of my food away and help her back to the car, but I drive too slow, still picturing her in the hard prairie light with a mouthful of mud.

Del spins the radio dial, finds a rock song with a heavy bass line, and she taps her fingers on her thigh in time. Her eyes tick around in her face like they're trying to see everything at once, until she closes them. She rests the back of her hand on my knee and I can feel the heat right through my jeans. Her palm is unnaturally smooth, and I wonder if it's hard for her to hold things, if they slip off that skin like it was vinyl. Looking at her makes it hard to think. Death is in her and through her and all around her, but she moves and breathes regardless.

By eight o'clock it's dark out. Del is asleep, and with no conversation and nothing but dark highway to look at, I get tired quick. I find a motel and pull off. Del stirs, lifts her head, and leans it down again.

"Why are we stopping?" she says.

"It's late. I'm too tired to drive anymore."

"I'm in a hurry."

"A few hours won't make a difference."

She doesn't answer but closes her eyes. I check in, park the car near our room and help her inside.

"Do you want to take the first shower?" I ask her.

"No," she says, but then she looks down at her clothes, smeared with mud.

She goes into the bathroom and closes the door. I stand outside in the dark and listen to the sound of the water against the bathtub, against her body. She showers for a long time, half an hour maybe, so that I start to wonder if something's happened to her. At last the water stops, and I sit at the foot of one of the beds and pretend to watch TV in the darkness. Del opens the door to the bathroom and steam and yellow light pour out around her like a magician's cloud of smoke. She is naked, standing up straight, and I see that she's taller than I thought, taller than I am. I look down at my feet and close my eyes to stop myself staring.

"It doesn't matter," she says. "I rinsed my clothes, and I wanted to let them dry."

She steps closer and I can smell her, mud and heat lightning, black pepper and rust, apples fermenting in the high grass, all of it compressed together. She pulls the covers off the other bed and crawls between the sheets. The darkness is filled with the smell of her.

Turning on her bedside lamp, she says, "You can sleep here if you want."

She says it the way you might offer to lend someone five dollars, and somehow that makes it crueler to say no. I want her to keep that pride. Besides, I don't know anyone who wouldn't want a hand to hold on their way out of this world, myself included. It doesn't seem like the kind of thing you should have to beg for.

I sit beside her on her bed and she pulls my hand onto her forehead and closes her eyes. On her chest, over her heart, is a fist-sized bruise, dark purple. The flesh there looks like it would be soft and wet to the touch, like pulp. Her body is marked with blisters, scratches, bruises, veins that look like they're trying to come through the skin. The wholeness of my own body, even with all its scars, suddenly seems unfair.

She slips a hand inside my shirt and moves her burning fingers across my chest. I stretch out on the bed, the two of us shoulder to shoulder, and we lie there for hours. Her body, where it touches me, is a razor. The hours of the night stretch and blend. I wake up next to her and find that I'm crying, that I'm clinging to her wasted body. She smoothes her palms along my back and whispers to me, and all it does is make everything hurt more. I want to chase the darkness out from under her eyes, breathe life back into her, fill her up with mud if that's what'll make it work. I've never known a woman more painful, but I want to touch her all the same.

I say, "Look, let me take you home. You're too sick to be doing this. We'll go together."

She shakes her head.

"Take a good rest, then," I say. "How do you expect to get better moving around all the time? Stay in bed a couple of days, why don't you?"

"I don't want to rest. Let's drive the whole way tomorrow."

"It's got to be another eighteen hours."

"Please. I'll pay you if you want, let's just go."

"For Christ's sake, don't get insulting."

She wakes me up at dawn, trailing her fingers along my cheeks, and I'd wager she didn't sleep the whole night. As soon as I'm dressed, she walks outside and gets in the car, and I don't argue.

By dusk my eyes feel like they're made of glass, but we're near the coast. I shake Del awake and ask her where she wants to go. She presses her hands against the window and squints into the darkness. "It all looks different than I remember it."

Whenever we pass someone on the street she calls out to ask for directions, and the people point and wave us along, if they answer at all. We turn onto a bigger road with cars buzzing past, and as soon as we do I can smell the ocean. Del shivers in the seat beside me and grips my knee. Against the skyline you can see the lights of a carnival turning on, first the Ferris wheel, then the booths, sending up a blaze of bulbs and neon to replace the fading sunset.

"This the place?"

"I don't know," she says. "I think so. It was just an empty boardwalk last time I was here."

She leans against me as we walk down the midway, our arms looped together. Del looks all around her, gawking as if she never saw a carnival before, like she fell asleep in her bed at home and woke up here and can't figure out what the hell happened in between. We come to an amusement stand and the barker starts in on me, "Win a prize for the pretty lady!" He's got to notice how she looks, but I guess carnies have seen just about everything. He smiles at her like she's Miss America, and I give him two dollars for a stack of baseballs to pitch at the milk bottles. I hate this game—they weight the bottles so that it's almost impossible to win—but I do all right, three bottles down.

"Anything in the bottom row," says the barker.

"Pick what you want," I say to Del.

She gets one of those glow necklaces and puts it on her head like a crown. The strange light makes her look almost normal. We buy an ice cream and a funnel cake and eat them next to the roller coaster.

"This is almost like a date," she says.

"I learned better than to date crazy girls like you; it's always trouble."

"Do you date dead girls? I bet that's even worse." She smiles, but it's not a real smile, and she starts crying.

"Come on, now," I say, and I put my arms around her and hold her head against my chest, green light from her glowing crown climbing up into my eyes. The roller coaster swoops over us, the people scream. The merry-go-round stops and a bunch of kids climb off and run past, laughing as they go. Del looks up and wipes her eyes with the back of her hand.

"Sorry," she says.

"Nothing to be sorry for."

"I thought I was going to make it."

"Who says you aren't?"

"I want to go down to the beach."

We find the stairs that lead us to the sand, and as soon as we take five steps the light and the noise from the carnival start to fade. I put my arm around her waist to help her walk. The sand is white and fine and cool as Christmas, and it'll turn your ankles if you're not careful. We go down to the water's edge, where the footing is better, where the waves sweep against our toes. Del takes her shoes off and throws them into the ocean before I can stop her.

She takes my hand and guides it in between the buttons of her shirt, over her breast, presses it against the bruised spot on her chest. The flesh is even softer than I'd imagined; my fingers sink into it until I can feel her bones through her skin, and below them the shuddering of her heart.

"This is what I feel all the time," she says, "only it's the whole world beating." She pushes my hand closer until I'm afraid my fingers will go right through the skin, and that heart sounds like it could devour me.

Del

For a moment, with Troy's hand against my chest, I can almost imagine a life all my own, almost understand how that

could be fulfilling. He holds me to him and I am alive wher-
ever his body touches me. But ghosts with my face surround
me, six other hearts echo my heartbeat. There is nothing I
can give him because nothing I have is mine.

I step away from him, across the sand. A moist breeze
skims my shoulders and I feel myself dissolve, as if the salt
air could unravel my genetic code like a piece of knitting.
Nature won't have me, won't let me buy my life with their
deaths. Aberrations, abominations, Nature wants us gone.
Who knew the world was so unforgiving, so eager to cull?

There are shells, says Helen, *don't cut your feet,* and
every shell touches the sole of my foot seven times. There is
nothing strange in this anymore, that she can choke to death
on her own blood while I sleep in a roadside motel, and yet
still be with me days later, whispering in my ear. *Walk into
the surf,* my sisters say, *the ground pulls out from underneath our toes.* The waves are sevenfold in their coldness,
the salt air seven times as pungent.

The water sings between my fingers, surges around my
knees and shins as they press into the sand. *Drink deep,* my
sisters say. This is where things crumble irrevocably, where
there is nowhere left to go. We'll become salt. We'll become
storm clouds on the water. And then emptiness, one to
seven to one to zero in the space of twenty-three years. Science will have nothing to do with us anymore, nor we with
it. We will be just a void in the cosmos, a dark place in the
sky where there was once starlight.

Acknowledgments

As I set out to write these acknowledgments I feel like I'm back in high school, trying to find the right words to inscribe in yearbooks. Let's hope I can do a better job this time around.

I have been fortunate enough to find other writers who have become both my trusted critics and my confidants. Mike, Cindy, Scott, Eric, Jen, Maggie, and Joe, for a decade of honesty, wine, and friendship, I cannot thank you enough. I'm amazed by your talent and resilience and count myself lucky that you took me in all those years ago. Kath and Gary, thank you for your keen eyes, your humor, and your advice. Tess, as much fun as we've had together, what I want to say most is *just send it out;* it's already more than finished, it's gorgeous. Maureen, where would I be without all those long walks in the park and late nights where we decoded every glory and flaw in the world of literature (and everything else)? I didn't know I could still find friends (and writers) like you this far along. June, thank you for being the person on the other end of the phone at just the right moment, to make me laugh at both the world and myself. And Kaethe— lady, what can I say? You've talked me through the most tangled parts of writing and of life, and I don't know how anyone can be simultaneously such a gifted artist and so humble. I will always be grateful for the day you stepped out of that car and into that cornfield.

I have also had more wonderful teachers than any one person deserves. I want to thank Mr. Earl Feigert, at Hickory Elementary School in Hermitage, Pennsylvania, who gave me my first creative writing assignments when I was in the third grade. It was an early chance to find out what I really love in life, and I'm grateful for it. Debbie Reaves not only taught me to analyze literature in a way that made it seem like an adventure, but also showed me what it meant to be a feminist in all the best senses of that word. Samantha Chang, Chris Offutt, and my other teachers at the Writers' Workshop provided much-needed support and a wealth of creative intelligence. Stephen Lovely gave me the opportunity to teach creative writing to high school students for nine years, and they in turn taught me more than I could have imagined. Thank you to Kevin Brockmeier—I feel blessed to have had a teacher who is such a master at creating both fairy tales and beautiful prose, and who has given me so much help and encouragement over the years. And Connie Brothers, I know you're not a writing teacher but I've learned more while walking with you to your next appointment than seems possible. Thank you.

For her help in the process of writing and publishing this book I want to thank my agent, Sarah Levitt, who stuck with me through the years, advocated for me, and gave me a good firm push when I needed it most. Thank you to Laura Van der Veer for giving me my chance and for her great edits, and to Annie Chagnot for her wonderful editing, her enthusiasm, and her help at every step along the way to completing this book. Special thanks to Zainab Adisa and her family for taking the time to read "All the Names for God" and offering me their cultural perspective. And to Elsie Byrde, for the translation of "About Prince Surprise" in *The Glass Mountain and Other Polish Fairy Tales*, which inspired the story "Anything You Might Want."

Finally, I want to thank those closest to me:

Langston, for not becoming famous before I even got my first book published. That would have been embarrassing.

Duncan, for always treating me as a serious artist, even when I resisted.

Andrea, thank you for taking time off from being superwoman to be my cheerleader whenever I needed one.

Marty, my one, true Magician. Thank you for being brave

enough to build a life made of magic, and encouraging me to do the same.

Thank you to my father, for filling my childhood with endless bedtime stories and always supporting my ambitions, even though they were so different from his own.

And to my mother: lover of words; teller of tales; my first, best writing teacher; and no mean writer herself.

ANJALI SACHDEVA'S fiction has appeared in *The Iowa Review, Gulf Coast, The Yale Review, Alaska Quarterly Review, The Literary Review,* and *The Best American Nonrequired Reading.* She is a graduate of the Iowa Writers' Workshop and has taught writing at the University of Iowa, Augustana College, Carnegie Mellon University, and the University of Pittsburgh. She also worked for six years at the Creative Nonfiction Foundation, where she was director of educational programs. She has hiked through the backcountry of Canada, Iceland, Kenya, and Mexico, and spent much of her childhood reading fantasy novels and waiting to be whisked away to an alternate universe. Instead, she lives in Pittsburgh, which is pretty wonderful as far as places in *this* universe go. This is her first book.

anjalisachdeva.com

ABOUT THE TYPE

This book was set in Caledonia, a typeface designed in 1939 by W. A. Dwiggins (1880–1956) for the Merganthaler Linotype Company. Its name is the ancient Roman term for Scotland, because the face was intended to have a Scottish-Roman flavor. Caledonia is considered to be a well-proportioned, businesslike face with little contrast between its thick and thin lines.